Praise for A

'Fascinating ... if one c
good novel is that the characters do not remain static
but are subtly transformed by events, then this
is a very good novel indeed'
Sunday Telegraph

'Credible, intriguing and admirably developed ...
a substantial and entertaining book'
Scotsman

'Perhaps the best work of fiction about modern
soldiering since the books of Leslie Thomas
and David Lodge'
Evening Standard

'Superbly crafted ... Intricate and compelling, it gives an
all-too-plausible glimpse at how espionage actually works'
Daily Mail

'Defiantly old-fashioned yet illuminating ...
gentlemanly entertainment'
Sunday Times

'He knows that world backwards and writes with
an understanding of human frailty that is rare'
Sunday Express

'Has all the virtues of a well-researched plot,
intelligent prose and topicality'
Literary Review

'This is a documentary novel that has the authentic feel of
a race against time. It might be unwise to miss it'
New Fiction Society

ACCIDENTAL AGENT

ACCIDENTAL AGENT

ALAN JUDD

**SIMON &
SCHUSTER**

London · New York · Sydney · Toronto · New Delhi

A CBS COMPANY

First published in Great Britain by Simon & Schuster UK Ltd, 2019
This paperback edition published by Simon & Schuster UK Ltd, 2019
A CBS COMPANY

1 3 5 7 9 10 8 6 4 2

Simon & Schuster UK Ltd
1st Floor
222 Gray's Inn Road
London WC1X 8HB

Simon & Schuster Australia, Sydney
Simon & Schuster India, New Delhi

www.simonandschuster.co.uk
www.simonandschuster.com.au
www.simonandschuster.co.in

A CIP catalogue record for this book
is available from the British Library

Paperback ISBN: 978-1-4711-5068-5
eBook ISBN: 978-1-4711-5069-2

Typeset in Sabon by M Rules
Printed and bound by CPI Group (UK) Ltd, Croydon, CR0 4YY

To Jo

Chapter One

Reflecting on it afterwards, it seemed to Charles Thoroughgood that the whole sad affair began with a wedding reception. The origins long pre-dated that, of course, germinating secretly in the characters and careers of the principal actors, but it was at that sunlit reception on the lawn of a large house in south-west London that it all began to unravel.

Or come together, depending on how you looked at it. There was, it turned out, a pattern in the carpet that Charles hadn't spotted because he wasn't looking. Even if he had looked, it would have seemed fanciful to perceive such an emerging shape. It was his failure, he had to admit afterwards; as chief of MI6 part of his job was to be alive to such possibilities but he had allowed familiarity and friendship, twin enemies of vigilance, to cloud his sight. Not to mention complacency and – harder to admit – age. The pattern was in the carpet all along but he did not see it until it was too late. Almost.

He later dated it to a precise moment at the reception, the first flickering indication that there might be a problem. The wide, red, wine-mottled face of a former colleague had grinned at him across a champagne glass and said, 'Must say, retirement's taught me what I long suspected.' He paused for Charles to respond.

Charles struggled. He remembered the man – one or two of his postings and MI6 Head Office jobs, a minor scandal in New Delhi that led to divorce, his retirement party a couple of years before. Everything except his name.

'That people have jobs to avoid work.' The red face creased in laughter, the eyes almost disappearing in folds of flesh.

Avoidance of work was something else Charles now remembered about the man. He had done his quota of that in a so-so career limited not so much by lack of ability as by lack of aspiration and a preference for the diplomatic drinks circuit over the hard graft of finding and recruiting useful agents. One of those officers who was always in or between meetings, another way of avoiding work. But the name – Jerry something? John? There were so many Johns.

'Of course, your own retirement must be coming up, isn't it? Unless MI6 chiefs can prolong themselves indefinitely, which I doubt, these days. I suppose

Gareth Horley will take over, will he? What he always wanted. Hungry Horley, we called him in Lagos. Always rushing off to the high commissioner with some titbit before telling his head of station. Usually a report that turned out to be exaggerated, putting it kindly. Mind you, with old What's-His-Face as head of station – old Thingy, you know, that madman – can't do names for the life of me these days – you couldn't blame Gareth. Jimmy Milton, that's it. Did you ever work with Jimmy? Mad as a hatter about security. Used to bury his house keys in his garden before going anywhere under alias. As if anyone claiming to live a blameless ordinary life in 123 Acacia Avenue wouldn't have the means for getting back into 123 Acacia Avenue when he got home. I remember one day when Jimmy . . .'

Charles tried to look interested without too obviously gazing across the lawn crowded with other wedding guests. He was recalling ever more about his interlocutor, but still not the name. A genial cove – a word the man would himself have used – helpful, friendly, dependable, limited, loyal. Above all, loyal, the most important quality in an intelligence officer. Lack of any other quality could be compensated for or worked around but lack of loyalty undermined everything. It was probably the most common, and therefore most underrated, quality among people in the Office. It was a given: you were part of the family, you could have rows and disagreements daily but loyalty, absolute loyalty, was taken for granted. Rightly, in almost every case. And therein lay its danger.

Interesting that the man should name Gareth Horley as his possible successor as chief. Charles had discussed his likely recommendation with no one apart from Sarah, his wife, and the cabinet secretary, to whom he answered. Gareth was director of MI6 operations, effectively Charles's deputy, promoted by him because he was everything that this nameless interlocutor was not – hard-working, with a good operational record of recruiting and running important agents, an effective bureaucrat who understood how to work Whitehall without appearing too manipulative, a charming, effective and amusing colleague. Granted, he wasn't universally popular in the Office, being seen – by his own generation in particular – as nakedly ambitious, a smiling assassin whose chief loyalty was to himself. But that was not incompatible with loyalty to the Office and to his country, and ambition was now regarded as creditable so long as it furthered the cause as well as the individual. It was different when Charles had joined decades before, when to call someone ambitious was a serious criticism. The trick then was to be ambitious without showing it; now, you were marked down on your annual assessment if you didn't display it. The change had favoured Gareth.

But no one was perfect and Charles was persuaded

that the Office would do better under Gareth than under any other in-house choice. He was also satisfied that his choice would have been the same even if he and Gareth had not been on friendly terms for years and had not, as younger officers, run operations together. Not that these days the choice of successor was any longer his; EU rules required that the post be advertised to outsiders and Whitehall might well decide that it would look more fashionably inclusive to have a woman, or someone from an ethnic minority or an out-to-grass politician to run Her Majesty's Secret Service. But his view would still carry informal clout because of his relations with the cabinet secretary and the various departmental permanent secretaries who would decide the shortlist before recommending it to the foreign secretary and prime minister. So long as he didn't make a mess of things in the meantime. Also, with Brexit the reign of EU rules was presumably coming to an end.

'One thing I wanted to ask.' The man lowered his voice and moved closer, with the exaggerated solemnity of a spaniel begging a biscuit. 'These negotiations, this Brexit stuff – I hope we're reporting on the buggers, their position papers, fallbacks and all that? Bloody well should be.'

It had become a frequent question since the Brexit referendum, easily answered. 'Off-limits as far as Whitehall is concerned. They wouldn't wear it. Spying on friends is politically more dangerous than spying on enemies. Anyway, the EU is so leaky we don't need to; it all comes out in the wash. Maybe it'll change after we've left.'

'But they're not our friends, they're trading partners who are also competitors. Anyway, countries don't have friends, they have interests. Can't remember who said that. Applies even more to intelligence services.'

Charles was relieved to spot Sarah's blue and white dress as she detached herself from the crowd and came across the lawn towards them. Luckily, he was spared the embarrassment of introductions. 'Robin,' she said, smiling and holding out her hand to the red-faced man, 'we haven't met since your retirement party. How's retirement treating you?'

'Sarah, how are you, lovely to see you. I was just saying to Charles, it's taught me what I've long suspected ...'

Charles relaxed. Sarah, a lawyer who was not in the Office herself, was unique in having married successive chiefs and so had long experience of the kind of social chit-chat required. Also, she had a rather better memory than Charles for names and people, many of whom she knew through her late husband. She knew too that they would all have a simplified version of her and Charles's history – youthful lovers at Oxford, rivalry with the man she later married, a child sent for adoption, decades of estrangement from Charles followed by reconciliation after the disgrace and death of her husband; and Charles's role in his downfall. Knowing that this was what they would all be thinking of while talking to her, she had felt awkward and self-conscious for months after she and Charles had married but the gradual realisation that most people were more interested in themselves than others had made things easier. Now, she knew that if she didn't let the past become a problem for her, everyone else would ignore it, even if they didn't quite forget. After a few minutes she said, 'Robin, much as you two would like to continue your Office gossip I'm afraid I have to grab Charles and force him to bid our farewells. He has to go back to work.'

Robin raised his eyebrows in mock, or perhaps genuine, dismay. 'What, working at weekends? Surely as chief you could get other people to do that for you?'

'Thank God you came,' Charles whispered as they walked arm in arm towards the marquee. 'I thought I was trapped there for the duration. How's it been for you?'

'I think I've got away with it so far. Just hope we can leave before I put a foot wrong. What time's this thing you're doing?'

His phone was vibrating in his pocket. He acknowledged the text. 'Okay if we leave in the next ten minutes.'

'I can't do that. I must stay a bit longer. You go off and I'll get a cab back.'

It was an Anglo-Indian wedding in the bride's parents' home in Wimbledon, a large Edwardian house with a garden the size of two tennis courts. Robin was there because he lived in the modest bungalow next door – 'The best my pension will pay for in this part of London. Not that you'll have to worry about that sort of thing, I suppose' – and Charles and Sarah because the groom, Daniel Adamson, was her godson. It was a colourful affair, the saris and costumes of the bride's family outshining and outnumbering Daniel's more soberly and uncertainly dressed relatives. Daniel, who had converted to Islam, wore a long green jacket edged with gold, his red beard trimmed and his hair cut. His bride, Akela, wore a flowing white dress, high-necked with long diaphanous sleeves and a see-through hood, the whole thing populated by what seemed to Charles to be sewn-in table-tennis balls. She smiled continuously but was generally quiet and looked nervous, unlike her parents, who were energetically gregarious and hospitable.

'But ten minutes is a bit soon,' continued Sarah. 'Can't it be longer? You must say goodbye to Deborah and everyone.'

'Everyone?'

'You know what I mean.'

Sarah was uncharacteristically brittle over anything to do with Daniel and his mother, Deborah, an old schoolfriend. She felt guilty over her self-perceived neglect of her godmotherly duties, though Daniel himself had never welcomed them.

'I'm forever on edge with Deborah and I don't really understand why,' she had admitted on their drive from Westminster to Wimbledon. 'We get on, we've never fallen out or fought over anything, there are no obvious issues. It's just that she's always so perfect in everything, always has been, which makes me feel I have to act up to her expectations – which I can't because I'm anything but perfect and it makes me nervous and I overdo it and it probably comes across to her as if I'm competing . . .' She paused. '. . . There was space for comment there.'

'You are perfect. It goes without saying.'

'I'm not and it doesn't, which is why it needs saying.'

'She's not exactly perfect where Daniel's concerned. She's all over the place with him.'

'That's because she's hyper-defensive, which makes it worse. She can't admit she doesn't like the way he's turned out, so we all have to pretend we don't notice, and I make extra efforts to be the godmother he plainly doesn't want so that she doesn't think I disapprove. And of course my efforts fail because he never has wanted them, so I stop trying for a while and then she says something and I renew my efforts, which are obviously insincere, and he goes on as before.'

'But converting to Islam and marrying a Muslim

seems to have introduced some discipline to his life, which must surely be a good thing.'

'Let's hope. Not that it's what Deborah would have wanted for her one and only, rich though they are. Still, she's putting a brave face on it and we have to keep telling her how pleased we all are for him, which of course she doesn't believe.'

Daniel's troubled past had cost Deborah and her then husband a deal of anxiety and money. His expulsions from successive private schools, usually couched in terms of recommendations for a specialist education more suited to his needs, culminated in his absconding from the last on the eve of examinations. He was eventually picked up by the police following an outbreak of rioting in Bradford, where he had been living rough. Charges relating to public disorder were not proceeded with and there followed a decade of unfinished courses, abandoned careers, temporary unskilled jobs, expensive stays in rehabilitation units and taxpayer-funded fresh starts. Eventually, following his parents' divorce, he completed a course that qualified him as a carpenter, funded by his father as part of the divorce settlement. He found work with a small building firm in south-west London and had been a convert to Islam for a year or so before telling his parents. He changed his name to Abdul-Salaam, met and married Akela and now worked for himself.

Her family had multifarious business interests but

were mainly food wholesalers. 'I get the impression he's more religious than his in-laws,' whispered Sarah, as they approached the marquee. 'Enthusiasm of the convert, I suppose. He's stopped drinking and all that whereas they obviously have no inhibitions. But they can't be over the moon about their beloved daughter marrying a mere carpenter rather than the scion of another wealthy Indian Muslim family. And one of Jewish origin at that, albeit non-practising. Deborah's lot just look baffled, don't they?'

'His sister-in-law, Anya, seems nice. She told me Akela is a Muslim name meaning wise. It had never occurred to me. I only knew it as the name of the leader of the Cub pack.'

Anya was younger than Akela and was a trainee lawyer with a City firm. She wore a brilliant blue sari and made valiant efforts with all the groom's guests. She was the only one to mention Charles's job.

'Of course, I have to believe everything my new brother-in-law tells me,' she had said, smiling, 'but I had a moment of doubt when he told me the head of MI6 was coming to a Muslim wedding. Is that allowed?'

Charles smiled back. 'Almost compulsory now. We employ Muslims, have done for decades though no one knew it. But this is my – our – first Muslim wedding.'

'I hope you feel safe?'

'Safer here than anywhere.'

11

They found Daniel just inside the marquee, sipping water and patiently receiving congratulations. His beard, grown since his conversion, was neatly squared off and his previously shoulder-length hair was cut above the ears. He smiled at their approach, something he would not have done before. 'No cloaks or daggers here for you two, I'm afraid. Unless you want to disappear into the rhododendrons.'

Sarah laughed. 'Might be misconstrued.'

As they elaborated on their congratulations, Charles's mind returned to his working lunch with Michael Dunton, director general of MI5, earlier that week. He and Michael lunched monthly on sandwiches and fruit juices, alternately in each other's offices. Charles, being like red-faced Robin of a generation for whom lunchtime drinking had been a sustaining prop for the rest of the day, deferred unprotestingly to the fashion for abstinence while secretly regretting it.

'One last thing,' Michael had said. 'Sarah has a godson, I believe, who is a recent Muslim convert?' They had dealt with all their other business, the usual run of incipient turf disputes, resource allocations and personnel issues that it was in their mutual interest to resolve before they became too serious.

Charles raised his eyebrows. Any item introduced

as 'one last thing' was rarely an afterthought. 'How did you know?'

'Facebook, apparently. Not that Sarah's on it, I'm told, but the godson's mother is and Sarah features on her page. Ditto young Daniel, of course, hence some of his associates, and it's them we're interested in. A couple of them, anyway. They've been recommending certain extremist websites to him, the sort that encourage self-starters to strike a blow for Allah with knife or vehicle, that kind of thing. No indication that he's about to oblige but they're saying that converts need to prove themselves and he doesn't seem to argue with it. I only mention it because we discovered your connection with him via Sarah via his mother and all the wedding stuff and the desk officer thought you should be aware of it.'

'He's quite right. Please thank him.'

'She also asked whether Sarah would be happy to meet her and talk about Daniel in case anything looks like developing. Assuming Sarah knows him better than you do?'

'She does, yes. I'm sure she would be happy to meet her.'

'Thanks. Gareth Horley seems to be behaving himself, I'm happy to report.'

There had been an episode some months before when Gareth's exasperation with what he saw as MI5 foot-dragging over a joint terrorist case that moved regularly between Luton and Islamabad had led him to speak frankly, as he had put it. Personally abusive and bureaucratically hostile were the words used by MI5's head of operations when she complained to Michael. There were two case officers, one from each service, with the agent under MI5 control in Luton, MI6 in Islamabad. Normally, such arrangements worked seamlessly, with the agent unaware of any distinction, but in this case he had complained to his MI6 case officer that the handler he met when in Luton seemed unresponsive to his requests and had apparently failed to act on some very specific intelligence about the meeting of a potential bombing team in a flat above a bookmakers'. That was half true, in that the date of the meeting passed while MI5 and the police were still discussing whether to intervene; but in fact the meeting hadn't happened and it turned out that MI5 had another source who had said it wouldn't. The section concerned, which did not know about the joint case, had not reported the non-event to MI6, nor had news of it reached the MI5 director of operations by the time Gareth rang her to complain.

'I confess to intemperance,' Gareth had said to Charles with a smile, 'and perhaps a few expletives undeleted.'

'But what really upset them was hearing what you'd said about them to GCHQ after you'd discovered that the meeting was cancelled.'

'Okay, take your point. Though on that occasion I was complaining not so much about this incident itself as the fact that it fitted a pattern of sluggish reporting and acting.'

'Because, it seems, they have other sources reporting in the same area, not all saying the same thing. They have reason to be cautious.'

Gareth held up his hands. 'Okay, okay, I shouldn't have spoken in those terms. Point taken. Must learn to button it.'

Now, when Michael mentioned the subject again, Charles was able to take a more relaxed view. 'Glad to hear you've had no more problems. He seems to have become better behaved all round.'

'Presumably he's aware that if he wants to succeed you he needs more friends than enemies.'

This was the first of several unprompted indications that others saw Gareth as Charles's potential successor. Either Charles's mind was easily read or Gareth's record spoke for itself. 'Could you work with him?'

The response was not immediate. 'Yes.'

'With reservations?'

'Allowances rather than reservations. Allowances for temperament and manner but respect for abilities and achievements and for his reputation for making waves and getting things done.'

A reputation for making waves was not always desirable in Whitehall, despite ritual worship at the altar of change, but it was good enough for Charles. He was aware that during his own tenure he had ignored various structural and administrative issues that others thought were important. For him, they were secondary to delivering the goods and, so long as the Office delivered – in terms of intelligence produced – he preferred not to think about them. Whitehall, he suspected, thought it time for a new broom. Avoiding unpalatable tasks was one of his weaknesses, he knew.

Now, at the reception, it was refreshing to find a friendly, if somewhat solemn, Daniel, not at all the potential extremist who worried MI5. 'We had a lovely chat with Akela,' said Sarah. 'She's charming.'

'Thank you. I'm sure she will be a very good Muslim wife, thanks be to Allah, peace and blessings be upon him.'

There was no trace of irony in his round freckled face. Hard though it was for the habitually secular to take religious avowals seriously, it was a welcome change from the sullen hostility of Daniel's pre-conversion youth.

'And we chatted to Anya, her sister, too,' said Sarah. 'She seemed very nice, quite a live wire.'

Daniel nodded. 'But less devout than Akela. You've seen I've changed my name. I have a Muslim name now.' He relieved his solemnity with a smile. 'I'm surprised – grateful – you could come. I didn't think you would, given Charles's job.'

'No reason why not,' said Charles. 'None at all.'

'You know I'm a carpenter now? Really enjoying it.'

'Good religious precedent.' Charles regretted his flippancy as soon as he said it.

Daniel had to think. 'Of course, the prophet Jesus. He's only a prophet in Islam. But an important one.'

'As in Judaism.'

Daniel's smile had gone now. 'The Jews – they're another matter. Them and the Americans.' He looked down, shaking his head.

'Your new family, your in-laws, seem very friendly and sociable,' said Sarah.

'They're not as observant as Akela but that's all right, we can cope. We will lead the simple lives of good Muslims.'

Charles's phone vibrated again. 'Excuse me a moment. Work. I'm on call.' He walked back across the lawn towards the rhododendrons. The call was one he had been expecting, from Gareth Horley. 'How did it go?'

'Couldn't be better. The crown jewels.' Gareth spoke slowly and quietly, unusually for him. It emphasised both his Welsh accent and his excitement. 'We've got them, the crown jewels. One of them, anyway.'

'Where are you?'

'About to leave Heathrow. Should be at Hyde Park in about half an hour. Are you coming?'

'Yes. You'll be there first but I should make it in time.' Hyde Park was the code name for the alternative Head Office outside Reading, a fully equipped emergency headquarters maintained in case a bomb or other event rendered the normal Westminster headquarters unusable. It was fully manned for that weekend.

'I'll draft a summary for you, headlines and bullet points only. We need to discuss Whitehall circulation. Number Ten, of course, but who else? Need to know and all that but in spades this time. If it got out it could scupper the Brexit negotiations. The big story is the red line, the one we were talking about on Thursday, the one you said was—'

'Save it till I get there.'

Chapter Two

The iron gates opened and one of the barriers was raised for Charles's ancient Bristol without his having to slow down more than enough to wave at the guards. They should have stopped and searched the car, of course, but they took pride in recognising the Bristol from a distance and he connived in their rule-breaking. Guarding anything was boring, relieved only by small pleasures. In his operational days he had broken rules and taken chances, albeit calculated, but as chief the opportunities were so limited as to make the occasional flouting, no matter how trivial, refreshing. It made him feel younger, which in turn made him feel it really was time to go.

The building codenamed Hyde Park had begun life as the nineteenth-century Palladian centrepiece of a country estate but successive incarnations as a school, a wartime military hospital, a mental asylum, a secret communications outpost during another war, a country club and a short-lived conversion to a semi-rural business centre had all but obliterated its architectural virtues. It was now converted into modern office suites with a communications centre in the cellars and an invisible array of oddly shaped aerials hidden in the attic. The gracious pillared entrance was cluttered by bulletproof glass and revolving doors. Locals assumed it was part of the nearby BBC monitoring service establishment at Caversham.

The car park, set for security reasons some distance from the house, was unusually full. At the far end were a coach, two army lorries and three police vehicles with people milling around them. But Charles took no notice as he docked the Bristol and hurried up the steps to the lawn that fronted the house. At the security doors he swiped in with his pass and took the lift to the third floor. His office was at the front of the building overlooking the main entrance and the pebbled drive to the distant gates. It was the only private office in the building, the rest being open-plan with meeting areas and glassed smaller offices for temporary use. Normally there would have been only a skeleton staff, plus the odd training course, but for that weekend it was fully manned with virtually every screen live and every desk occupied. Notwithstanding which, the atmosphere was relaxed and chatty. The level of chatter subsided like the trough of a wave as he passed each row of desks, but people smiled and looked up expectantly.

After checking his screen and not finding Gareth's promised summary, he told Jenny, his secretary, that he would be down with Gareth and set off for the first floor, using the stairs this time. There, he found Gareth's desk was occupied not by Gareth but by Sonia, head of assessments.

'Don't worry, I'm not trying to take over operations,' she said. 'Just leaving Gareth a note.'

'Makes a change to see anyone doing anything with pen and paper.'

'Quicker than screens but no one realises it.'

He and Sonia went back a long way. She was about five years younger than him and had started out as a secretary, in the days when secretaries were plentiful. Through working together as she rose through the ranks he had learned to trust her judgement and discretion; later she had been instrumental in securing his reinstatement in the Office after expulsion and arrest. He was responsible for her recent promotion to a senior position. Although publicly respectful of his status, familiarity meant she was not awed and could be trusted to speak her mind, which was one of the reasons he had pressured the reluctant HR director into promoting her.

'You'll probably find him in the control room,' she said. 'He was ringing them every two minutes to check on something.'

'Has he told you anything of his trip?'

'No but I've seen a summary in draft.'

'He hasn't sent it to me yet.'

'He hasn't sent it to anyone but he left it on his screen when he shouldn't have. So of course I closed it for him.' She smiled. 'After reading.'

'Seems very good, from what he told me.'

'So it seems.' She ceased smiling. 'We should talk about it.'

They looked at each other for a moment. Charles nodded.

The control room was on the first floor, off the balcony overlooking the entrance hall. It had about a dozen screens monitoring entrances and vulnerable points of the building, all switching angles every few seconds. The security staff, who were not uniformed, followed them in silence, occasionally intervening to change angle or revert to a previous shot. A telephone rang and was answered in a hushed tone. The silence, Charles suspected, was partly because Gareth Horley was standing just inside the door, his hands in the pockets of his jeans, looking on. He usually wore jeans on his Brussels trips, along with slim brown shoes from Tricker's of Jermyn Street – a fact he had twice mentioned to Charles – a white T-shirt and an expensive brown leather jacket. With his tanned regular features emphasising the blue of his eyes and his dark hair edged with grey, he looked every inch a confident, successful man of middle age travelling for a mixture of business and pleasure, which was the impression intended. He smiled as Charles approached and made way for him.

'Good trip, then?' said Charles.

'Fantastic trip. He told me their bottom line. Agreed at the EU Commission meeting on Thursday. Naturally, they're not going to reveal it to us in the negotiations but they would settle for it if they can't get us to up our public offer to theirs.'

'Sure it's the real thing?'

'Everything else he's said has checked out.'

They spoke in lowered voices. Charles patted Gareth on the shoulder. 'Well done.'

'It's so sensitive, this, more than anything else he's told us. We've got to be very careful with distribution. Number Ten might not want even the negotiating team to know in case by their manner or what they say or don't say they give it away. Remember that Ames and Hansen business.'

Aldrich Ames was a CIA officer who had spied for the Russians. In conducting the damage assessment for MI6, Charles had long sessions with the FBI team doing the same for the Americans. The nature of their questions, their keen interest in some areas and their unaccountable lack of it in others had led him to conclude that they believed they had another spy, but didn't want to admit to it and didn't yet know who or where. The spy turned out to be Hansen, an FBI officer as damaging as Ames. 'Let me see it before you talk to the Foreign Office.'

'I'll finish it off later this afternoon. Just thought I ought to show my face here as I'm in.'

'No sign yet?'

'Any time now, should be.' As Gareth spoke one of the screen-watchers called the supervisor over. She said something to the others, who switched their monitors to one of the rear approaches to the building, a gravelled track that led to high locked gates on the far side of the park bordering a public lane and a wood. Two men were climbing the gates. Charles and Gareth moved farther into the room to get a better view of the screens.

Then came the sound of smashing glass, followed by a shout from the security guard by the cubicles in the entrance hall and then two shots in rapid succession, very loud. Everyone in the control room turned away from the screens to look. The security guard was spreadeagled on the floor and a man wearing a grey suit and carrying a pistol was pressing buttons on the entrance control desk. Another man wearing a raincoat and carrying a sledgehammer ran towards the screened-off office where visitors' passes were issued, raising his hammer. The woman behind the screen tried to get off her chair but slipped beneath the counter onto the floor a second before the man swung his sledgehammer with both hands at the glass door to the side of her office, smashing it. Some control room staff got up from their desks, others sat staring. The supervisor ran to her own desk and pressed the alarm, a harsh jangling that rang throughout the building. Outside, two Land Rovers accelerated abreast of each other from the car park towards the broad steps leading up to the entrance. They slowed as they reached the steps but continued up them, jolting and bouncing, then accelerated again across the terrace and into the entrance. A number of black-clad, hooded men carrying sub-machine guns jumped out of each and ran in through the glass cubicles, which were all now open.

Charles and Gareth flattened themselves against the wall as the control room staff disintegrated in panic. The supervisor shouted into the microphone on her desk, 'There is an incident in the building. Stay where you are! All staff stay where you are!' Before she had finished one of her team, a man, shouted into another microphone, 'Building under attack! Intruders in the building! Evacuate the building! Evacuate now!' Several of the staff ran out of the control room onto the balcony, where they stopped as if suddenly frozen as the intruders split into two groups and ran up the curving stairs on either side. A couple of the control room staff stayed at their desks looking to the supervisor, who was shouting 'They must stay where they are!' at the man with the other microphone, who, oblivious to her, was shouting into it again, 'Do not use the lifts! Lifts not working! Evacuate! Evacuate!' There were more shots.

'We'd better get out of the way, leave them to it,' said Charles. He and Gareth slipped out into the corridor away from the balcony. The first office on the left was unlocked and empty. From the window they could look across to the two Land Rovers parked outside the entrance, their doors open but no one visible.

Gareth locked the door. 'Presumably you're a prime target, if they recognise you.'

'Just as well I'm not in my office.'

'Would they know which it is?'

'Probably not.'

The alarm stopped clanging, though in the silence that followed seemed to go on ringing. There was what sounded like heavy breathing in the microphone. A woman's voice said, 'Intruders . . . intruders . . . intruders on first floor east wing. Staff in east wing must . . . all other staff must evacuate by staircase number one west.' The alarm resumed, then stopped again. A man's voice said, 'Response team due in three minutes repeat three minutes. Remain in your offices and lock your doors. Repeat remain—' His voice became strangulated and the microphone made a noise as if it had been banged against something. In the park outside four Range Rovers raced up the drive from the main gate. Like the Land Rovers, they bumped up the steps and disgorged armed men, also in black but helmeted and wearing flak jackets signifying that they were police. There was more shooting.

Charles was looking out of the window. 'One of them's fallen over. That was his gun going off.'

Gareth leaned against the desk, smiling, his arms folded. 'Great. Boys in blue doing their usual stuff. And the control room helpfully broadcasting to the attackers where they are, where everyone else is going and when the cavalry's coming. Worth doing, don't you think? Confirms what we suspected: bloody chaos.'

'Lessons learned?'

'Apart from all that, no adequate defences against unauthorised vehicles getting close, possibly packed with explosive. Security booth reinforced glass easily broken. No adequate second barrier once they're through it. Control room all over the place, as we saw, despite being warned to expect it. And that's just what we witnessed. Another twenty minutes till final whistle, so there'll be plenty more.'

'You were right about doing it.' Charles was still looking out of the window. The security guard who had supposedly been shot was smoking a cigarette and chatting to the policeman who had fallen over. The policeman was pointing out where his bullets would have gone had his gun not been loaded with blanks. The exercise had been Gareth's idea, to test how Head Office might respond to a marauding attack. No one had tried it before; there had been hostage exercises, aircraft hijack exercises, tube train exercises, even ship seizure exercises, but no one had staged a marauding attack against an undefended government office. The head of security had opposed it, partly on the grounds that security staff were not trained or equipped to deal with such an event and partly, perhaps, because Gareth had proposed it. Charles had been in two minds but agreed when soundings indicated that there would be no shortage of volunteers to staff the reserve office on a Saturday and be part of the fun, as they saw it; partly, also, because anyone planning such an attack on an MI6 building was unlikely to wait for it to prepare itself. The head of security, MI5's head of physical security, people from the Home Office, senior police officers and the Special Forces liaison officer were all observing in different parts of the building. 'Wash-up at six?' Charles asked. 'Time for a quick chat about your report afterwards or would you rather do it in Head Office tomorrow?'

'Tonight would be better, if you don't mind. Headlines only. I need to get my notes into my safe and Suzanne's not expecting me back until later anyway. Big lunch do tomorrow and she'll take a gun to me if I spend another Sunday in the office. It won't be blanks, either.'

That suited Charles. Sarah had said she wanted to do a couple of hours' work that evening on an insurance case and they had agreed they would drive down to their Cotswold house late that night to spend Sunday there. Each had promised the other there would be no work.

Sarah was already working on her case when he got home, papers spread across the kitchen table. 'Good idea,' she said when he told her he was going into the office for an hour. 'I get more done when you're not here.'

'You got away from the wedding unscathed?'

'Only after prolonged farewells to Deborah. She's putting a very brave face on it all. Not just the marriage but Daniel's future. She's desperate to see him properly settled.'

'I got the impression he thinks he is, since his conversion.'

'Not in his mother's eyes, he isn't. She means a partnership in Deloitte or KPMG or something. She never wanted to be the carpenter's mum.'

'His sister-in-law looked a more likely prospect for that sort of thing.'

'That makes it worse.'

The new Head Office was in Westminster's Smith Square, a three-minute walk from their terraced house in Cowley Street. The building had previously served as Conservative Party headquarters, then as the European Union's London office, a minor but pleasing irony given what Charles was going there to discuss. It was too small to house more than a portion of MI6's Head Office staff and MI5's assessment of its physical security vulnerabilities had resulted in an unsightly periphery of heavy steel barriers. But it was not Croydon, where the much-reduced Service had been sent following the events that had led to Charles's unexpected recall and the downfall of his predecessor. That the rest of Head Office was distributed throughout various central London buildings was undeniably a disadvantage but returning to Westminster was essential. Despite all the advantages of modern communications, nothing compensated for physical proximity to the centres of power and regular access to those who occupied them.

Gareth's office, like Charles's, looked into the leafy upper branches of the plane trees in the square. Gareth was already at his desk, newer and grander than Charles's own. Charles had kept one of the very few Century House grade-four desks that had survived from the Cold War decades, a symbolism that did not, he knew, escape notice. Nor, in some cases, silent censure; but that didn't bother him.

'So, Timber Wolf delivered?' he said, sitting opposite Gareth.

Gareth turned aside from his screen and keyboard. 'Big time.'

'Headlines?'

'Plenty of negotiation mood music, bickering behind the seemingly united front, Poland and Hungary threatening to cut up rough, Nordics becoming more cautious. The big thing is the financial bottom line, which is higher than we thought.'

'Sub-sources?'

'The negotiating team, all of them. They all talk to him. Not all at once, nor do all of them tell him everything, but they all gossip or complain and he puts it all together.'

Timber Wolf was Gareth's source in the EU Commission, reporting on Brexit negotiations from the other side. A Dutch former diplomat whom Gareth had befriended while running the MI6 Geneva station, Timber Wolf had resigned from the Dutch foreign service to join the Commission as part of the policy development team. Although a permanent EU civil servant, he had remained an Anglophile and he and Gareth had kept up their friendship on a purely personal basis. Over the years there had been a family skiing holiday and occasional visits and dinners. Their friendship had been unaffected by the EU referendum, following which Timber Wolf began to be indiscreet about EU thinking. His indiscretions soon blossomed from office gossip into intelligence and had elevated their personal relationship into a professional one.

Such, at least, was the case so far as Gareth was

concerned. Charles was uneasy. Timber Wolf was not a recruited agent. Although he knew he was talking to an intelligence officer and would – or should – assume that anything he said of intelligence or diplomatic interest would be reported, that did not make him a secret agent, secretly reporting to a brief. He would surely, Charles had argued, have spoken in exactly the same terms to any foreign official with whom he had a long-standing personal relationship. In other contexts conversational indiscretions and gossip might amount to intelligence but in the free-flowing, relatively open culture of Brussels officialdom, they did not. The Joint Intelligence Committee had not mandated the EU as an intelligence target for MI6. Nor should Timber Wolf have been allocated a code name, as if he were an agent whose identity merited protection.

Gareth had done this off his own bat while Charles was on leave, issuing to Whitehall customers intelligence reports drawn from what Timber Wolf told him. Eagerly received in Whitehall as the Brexit negotiations spluttered on, they had garnered praise for Gareth and MI6, and would doubtless be remembered when the time came to choose a successor for Charles. Charles himself was congratulated on his return from leave as if it were a significant MI6 achievement. Both these factors had made it all the more difficult for him to refute or countermand what Gareth had done. It would have been difficult enough anyway, given their friendship and their history of successful joint casework, but the fact that everything Timber Wolf had so far reported appeared to check out made it all the more so. He had been careful not to fall out with Gareth over it but it was the closest they had ever come to open disagreement. He had concluded that the best way to ensure control of the case was to involve himself more closely. He had also, discreetly, asked Sonia to look at it.

'Are you absolutely sure,' he had pressed Gareth, 'that our customers understand that Timber Wolf is a loyal EU official who believes in ever-closer union leading to a United States of Europe and may not regard what he's telling you as secret or damaging? That he doesn't see himself as a spy?'

'Absolutely sure. I stressed from the start that these memos I'm issuing are not so much secret intelligence as what used to be called "deep chat". If you remember the days when diplomats used to be really good at talking to foreigners rather than to London or their screens.'

'And have you made them aware of the political embarrassment if it got out that he's talking to you like this and you're reporting it? Even though you're calling them memos rather than reports, it would still be dastardly MI6 Brits spying on the innocent, kindly and cuddly EU.'

'Absolutely they're aware. They always are, aren't

they? Terrified of embarrassment rather than simply refusing to be embarrassed. Anyway, it's kept very tight. Those memos can only be opened by named officials.'

Now, midway through a Saturday evening, sitting in Gareth's office with the lighting subdued and the plane tree leaves rustling in the breeze, Charles had once more to suppress his doubts. If what Gareth's draft memo said about the EU's bottom line was true, it was truly important. Lower than what the EU hinted at in public, it was still significantly higher than British estimates of what would be an acceptable compromise. There were important public policy implications for what the country could afford, as well as immediate presentational issues. 'Who's this going to?' he asked.

Gareth read aloud the list of addressees in Number Ten, the Cabinet Office, the Foreign Office and the Department for Exiting the EU. 'Longer than it was when I first started issuing them. More ministerial private offices. Ministers have heard about the case and are gagging to see the reports.'

'That's what worries me. People talk. And internally here?'

'As before. Just our directors and main board members.'

'Assessments?'

Gareth's eyes went back to his screen. 'Head of Assessments. Yes, she's here.'

Charles wasn't convinced that Sonia really had been on the distribution. She would be now. There was a long-standing antipathy between her and Gareth, dating back to an affair he had had, or half-had, or not had – according to him – with a girlfriend of hers, who had since left. More importantly, it was the task of Assessments to assess reports, whether they were true, whether they were timely, whether they met customers' requirements, whether they were supported by other reporting or whether they merely replicated what was already available through open sources. Assessments also had the right, in a change forced through by Charles in the wake of earlier security failures, to conduct assessments of agents – were they reliable, what were their motives, did they have direct access to what they reported, was their access oral, documentary or other visual, who were their sub-sources? In essence, who had said what, to whom, when, where, who else was there?

There had been several cases in which Gareth, whose job it was to enhance the production of intelligence, had been frustrated by what he called Sonia's meddlesome negativity. She, in turn, had complained that he was too gung-ho, too much inclined to uncritical acceptance and over-promotion of the product. 'The Salesman,' she called him, when talking to Charles. She shared some of Charles's earlier doubts about the Timber Wolf reporting.

'Great stuff, eh?' said Gareth with a smile when Charles handed him back the draft memo. 'Not bad for half a weekend's work.'

Interesting if true, was what Charles wanted to say, recalling the old Foreign Office put-down. Instead, he nodded. 'Great stuff indeed. Well done.'

Chapter Three

Charles was setting out Sarah's breakfast tray when Sonia rang them at precisely nine o'clock on the Sunday morning. It had rapidly become a convention of their recent marriage that he took Sarah breakfast in bed – boiled egg, toast, fruit, tea – on Sunday mornings, the only day when she was not up first. They were in her house in the hamlet of Swinbrook in Oxfordshire, overlooking the valley of the River Windrush. He was still in his dressing gown, gazing at the slow river while waiting for the kettle to boil. The eruption of the phone jerked him out of a pleasing vacancy.

'Hope I haven't woken you?'

'No, no, we're up and about.'

'I never ring anyone before nine in the morning or after ten in the evening.'

'Quite right.' He removed the kettle from the Aga before it began to whistle.

'Have you read the latest Horley blast? It came last thing last night.'

'No, but I saw it in draft and discussed it with him in the office yesterday evening. He was pretty excited about it.'

'Not surprised he was working late.'

'As were you, by the sound of it.' She must have seen it on her secure laptop at home.

'Funny thing is, the more I think about early retirement the harder it is to let go. I feel the opposite of demob-happy. We should talk about it. Gareth's email, I mean.'

'Fine. I haven't looked at my diary for tomorrow but we should be able to fit something in.'

'Today, I mean. I'm worried about it and I'd sooner discuss it outside the office. I feel I could be franker, somehow. I could drive over now if you're not too busy. Paul's at home, so he can walk the dogs.'

'It's quite a journey for you, isn't it? Unless it's really that urgent.' She lived in Hertfordshire but he was thinking of Sarah's reaction. Although she liked Sonia and knew how indebted Charles was to her, Sunday was the day they promised to each other; no work, no engagements.

'It is important. Which for me inevitably makes it seem urgent. Well, there is some urgency, actually. Genuinely. Anyway, it's a nice morning for a drive and it's ages since I've driven farther than the station. But if you've got something else arranged ...'

'No, no, it's fine. Come for lunch.'

'Coffee. I don't want to mess up the whole day for you both. I'll come for coffee.'

By the time she arrived it was warm enough to sit out on the terrace. Sarah had taken the news calmly, with well-concealed resignation, and had driven off to a garden centre the other side of Burford. Charles had Gareth's memo on his secure laptop and had read it three times. Sonia, despite looking relaxed in jeans and trainers and a T-shirt advertising a canine charity, was businesslike.

'I understand why you promoted Gareth. His operational record is seriously good and he's done some good things as director of ops and production. I'm not one of those who think you promoted him just through cronyism and the fact that you ran a couple of cases together.'

'Is that what people are saying?'

'One or two, no more. It's not a big issue. People can see he's effective and intelligent and a breath of fresh air after his predecessor. Nor do I have any personal issues with him despite how he behaved with my friend Jane, though I know you think I do.' She smiled. 'But I do think he might have personal issues with me, oddly enough. He never looks me in the eye and if I say something in a meeting he responds to someone else, as if they've said it.'

'Perhaps he's frightened of you.'

'I can't believe I frighten anyone.'

She did, though Charles had given up trying to persuade her of it. She was quiet, calm, self-possessed, rational, always mistress of her subject and nearly always right.

'The point,' she continued, 'and the reason I'm spoiling your Sunday, is that I'm worried about Gareth and Timber Wolf. I'm not convinced we're getting the full story. Or that we're getting the right story. If there is one.'

A heron got up from the bank of the Windrush, turned slowly and glided upstream. From the ridge on the far side of the valley came the sound of motorbikes on the A40. Her words provoked in Charles a simultaneous desire to argue and an unwelcome reminder of his own half-formed thoughts. Equally unwelcome was the thought that it should not have taken someone else's words to get him to acknowledge his doubts.

'I'm mentally taking a deep breath in saying this. Perhaps we both should.' Sonia paused, her eyes on his. 'Waiting for the exercise to get going yesterday, I read Timber Wolf's electronic file, what there is of it. I should have read it before. Have you read it?'

'No. I only know what Gareth has said about Timber Wolf.'

'Me too until yesterday, with less excuse than you. Gareth says on file that he has known him since Geneva, which he left six years ago. After that they kept in touch but vaguely, Christmas cards and all that, though Gareth never recorded him as a registered foreign contact as he should have done. Still less did he log him as any sort of source on any subject, conscious or unconscious. This despite the fact that Gareth now gives the impression that they'd seen quite a bit of each other since Geneva, with frequent contacts, at least one family holiday, dinners and so on.'

'That's what he told me.'

'In fact, there's no record on file of their actually meeting until after the Brexit referendum when Timber Wolf suddenly pops out of the woodwork and they have a couple of lunches in London, where Timber Wolf's visiting the EU office. Then there's a long weekend together *en famille*, with a bit of skiing in France. After the referendum and the lunches, note. Nothing before. During the holiday Timber Wolf begins dropping pearls of high-level EU gossip into Gareth's lap. After all those years of nothing to report.'

'Maybe there was nothing to talk about before then, no Brexit, no pearls, no gossip, no big issue.'

'Possibly. But also no lunches, no family get-togethers, no skiing *à deux*, no intimate professional revelations until the run-up to Brexit negotiations. So far as the record shows, Timber Wolf doesn't exist as any sort of source until he leaps fully formed out of the Alpine mist. Though Gareth does do a later note to say that they've been in touch all along.'

'Are you suggesting he doesn't exist, that Gareth's invented him?' Invented sources were not entirely unknown.

'Not at all. He checks out, he's real enough, his job is what Gareth says it is. But it's quite a coincidence, don't you think, that he's been in this sensitive EU Commission role ever since he left Geneva without once, we are asked to believe, being in the least indiscreet? Until, following the referendum and in the run-up to negotiations, he's suddenly Gareth's big buddy, volunteering secrets.' She shrugged. 'Maybe it's also a coincidence that Timber Wolf turns out to be on friendly terms with an FCO friend of mine who runs the UN desk. They too knew each other from Geneva and have kept in touch, I think a little more frequently than Gareth and Timber Wolf. They've met for drinks and the odd meal a couple of times since the referendum and not only has Timber Wolf dropped him no pearls but he has specifically said he can't discuss work now that their masters are on opposite sides of the negotiating table. And nor has he.'

'Perhaps he keeps his pearls for Gareth because he thinks Gareth is closer to the centre of power and that therefore anything he tells him is more likely to get through to the right people.'

'Perhaps. And perhaps he's also doing it with no expectation of pearls in return. There's certainly nothing in Gareth's write-ups to indicate a two-way conversation with all the trading you'd normally expect. So why is he doing it?'

'He's not paid, is he?'

'No. And yes. Not officially.' She hesitated. 'No names no pack drill. All right?' Charles nodded. 'I've a friend in Accounts. I took the opportunity to glance over Gareth's expense claims for his Brussels trips. She didn't show me sources, mind, I just happened to be in the room when ...'

'Of course.'

'Well, the best hotels, it goes without saying. And lavish lunches or dinners with Timber Wolf – they meet as old friends in public. Also, very generous expenses paid to Timber Wolf, unspecified but described as travel, accommodation etc. Well into five figures over five meetings. This despite the fact that Timber Wolf lives in Brussels.'

'Does he sign for these expenses?'

'No. I guess Gareth would say it's undignified to demand chits of an old friend, put a delicate relationship at risk and so on.'

Charles leaned forward, elbows on the garden table, hands clasped. 'So. Timber Wolf takes money for expenses he can't have incurred, knowing it comes from an intelligence service. In return, he passes confidential information, which he must assume will be passed by his intelligence service interlocutor, to his government, which is the other party to the negotiations. He does this because – well, we don't know why. For friendship and old times' sake, if Gareth is to be believed. Perhaps money comes into it, unstated by either party but implicitly acknowledged.' He sat back again and folded his arms. 'Sounds to me like a recruitment in all but name. We've done a lot of those. And we've also lost good cases by spelling out to them what they're doing just so that someone in Head Office can tick a box to say that this is a fully recruited conscious source. Not everyone likes to be confronted with the reality of what they're doing and maybe Timber Wolf is one of those.'

'But motivation and degree of consciousness should always be made clear on the file. Used to be, anyway, when there were proper files.' Sonia, like Charles himself and others of their generation, believed something was lost with the transfer to screens. 'There's nothing about either in Timber Wolf's screen file.'

'But there should be. There are boxes for it, aren't there? Doesn't anyone check?' In paper-file days there were registries staffed by middle-aged women who had seen everything in their time and were unafraid to badger officers, no matter how senior, who neglected their files. 'How has Gareth been able to buck the system?'

'By being so senior. He's in charge of all operations, what he says goes, what he does goes. It would be just the same if it were you getting – or claiming to get – intelligence from an old friend. No one would query how you reported it simply because you're the chief. I think you sometimes overlook that.'

Charles found his coffee cup empty again. She shook her head at his offer of more and he poured the dregs for himself. 'You say "claiming" to get intelligence. Are you implying that you think he's making it up?'

'Not quite. There's no evidence that he is. It all chimes with FCO and other reporting and with what eventually comes out in the media. My worry is whether most of it really counts as intelligence. It certainly counts in our report production figures – he's counted all his memos as five-star reports.'

That was not a surprise. Gareth had a history of playing the numbers game. In both the overseas stations he headed before promotion to management in London he had energetically boosted the station's reporting figures, quietly getting rid of officers who failed to produce. Charles had known this when promoting him but the results had justified Gareth's ambition and self-promotion. Charles had failed to play the numbers game when heading a station, arguing that quality was more important than quantity, that a single report that changed government policy or saved billions was worth more than hundreds that did no more than contribute to existing thinking. Right but naïve, he came to realise, suspecting that his strategy had contributed to his own early retirement some years before under the newly out-sourced HR regime.

'But this latest report surely counts as intelligence,' he said. 'I mean, you can't say that advance knowledge of the EU bottom line isn't hugely significant?'

'Of course it is. It's intended to be.' She looked out across the valley. 'You chose well, coming here.'

'It's really Sarah's. She chose well.'

She looked back. 'My worry is that Gareth might be a fabricator.'

This was perhaps the second most serious charge that could be laid, after the betrayal of agent identities, the sin against the Holy Ghost of espionage. Its consequences, political and other, were inevitably serious and long-lasting, a devaluation of the intelligence currency. 'I'll make some more coffee,' said Charles.

She followed him into the kitchen. 'My suspicions were first aroused during a course at the Castle.' The Castle was the Service's south-coast training establishment. 'Gareth gave the final address. He talked about the evolving political environment, the changing Whitehall culture and how our reporting priorities might change post-Brexit. He didn't give any detail of the negotiations but gave the kind of succinct summary you would expect from a good FCO briefing. Then a week later I read the report he issued following his latest meeting with Timber Wolf. It was virtually the same, word for word, and I thought, are these Timber

Wolf's words or Gareth's? Is he putting his own words into Timber Wolf's mouth?'

That was not unknown, deliberate or otherwise, especially in political reporting where the facts were known but interpretation and nuance were often what gave meaning. Sometimes it was simply a question of unconscious over-interpretation. 'He doesn't record their meetings?'

'I suggested that but he said that Timber Wolf would be insulted, not in keeping with their confiding friendship and anyway it might make him more cautious. He doesn't need to know, I said, but that got Gareth onto his high horse – "I'm not messing around with all those toys and tricks at my stage of career, surely you're not suggesting that after all these years of doing it I can't be trusted to report accurately what someone says to me?"' She did a passable imitation of Gareth's Welsh accent, heightened whenever he was irritated or excited. 'You can see why he doesn't like me.'

'Perhaps I should ask him myself. I could say it's essential that we're able to assure ministers of the exact words of the sub-sources Timber Wolf is quoting.'

'He might think you don't trust him.'

'But he'd have to do it. Refusal would look suspicious. It's all in the interests of absolute accuracy. I could say I've had a request from Number Ten.'

'And if he still refuses?'

'Then he's off the case. I'd take over, see Timber

Wolf myself.' Sonia stared at him as the coffee percolated, assessing his seriousness. There was no one else serving with whom he could discuss a fellow director in this way. 'Less dramatically, I could suggest he takes you along to the meetings.'

'I tried that, tentatively, saying it would strengthen the product when I'm discussing it in Whitehall if I could say I'd had it from the horse's mouth. But he went off the deep end – uniquely personal relationship, Timber Wolf would clam up in front of anyone else, take offence, feel he was being treated as a spy. All of which may be true.'

'I can see why he doesn't like you.'

'And after that he suggested I take a look at the current favourable terms for early retirement, eighty per cent funded by the Treasury. They're not going to last very long, he said. Is that right?'

'I'd close them tomorrow if I thought it would keep you.'

'I won't go until this is sorted out.' They took their coffees back out onto the terrace. The breeze had lessened, making the A40 less audible. 'One more thing, while we've still got Gareth on the dissecting table, dating from his time as head of the Geneva station. Do you remember Ian Catsfield?' Charles did not. 'A probationer under Gareth. A nice boy, rather academic, more analyst than operator. He and Gareth were chalk and cheese. Gareth asked him to cultivate an Iranian scientist who had access to Iranian nuclear. But after a few meetings the Iranian didn't want to see any more of Ian. Maybe he'd been warned off him, or warned off Westerners in general. Gareth wasn't impressed. He then got Ian to take on one of his own recruited cases, a Lebanese with terrorist connections. It had never been very productive and became less so under Ian. When Gareth asked why Ian said he didn't trust the agent, that he was in it for the money and cooking up any old story he thought we would swallow. Gareth took the case back and the product improved – surprise, surprise. The upshot was that Gareth recommended that Ian's probation should not be confirmed and he was sacked. The Office found him a job – with the Department of Health, I think – but he later left that for a think tank.

'Well, it now appears – in these litigious times – that Ian is involved with lawyers and is claiming unfair dismissal on the grounds that he should have been given a second chance under another boss, that Gareth only gave him dead-end tasks and exaggerated the intelligence product of his own cases. I suspect his think tank, which is pretty left-wing, has put him up to it. So that's another thing camping on Gareth's screen at the moment.'

Gareth hadn't mentioned it. Neither had the legal advisor who sat on the board and with whom Charles had weekly solo meetings, as with all his directors.

Sonia held up her coffee cup as if toasting him. 'Just wanted to get your week off to a good start.'

Back in London that night Charles went through all the Timber Wolf reports. By the time he had finished it wasn't only the possibility of fabrication that worried him.

Chapter Four

'The foreign secretary is delighted, as you can imagine. Very enthusiastic. Even allowing for the fact that enthusiasm is his default position, he's more than usually enthusiastic about this.' Robin Woodstock, Foreign Office permanent secretary, glanced at their fellow lunchers in the Travellers Club. 'I'll stick to two courses but you go ahead if you want pudding or cheese or anything.' He raised a hand to someone on another table. 'You know, when I joined the Foreign Office it was almost de rigueur to belong to this place but looking round now I can see only two colleagues, both retired. Mind you, you and I are part of a rapidly dwindling minority in Whitehall to acknowledge lunch at all. They all eat sandwiches at their desks now, don't they, still staring at their screens? Fortunately, the foreign secretary is enthusiastic about lunch, too. Another of his default positions. Pity Gareth Horley isn't around to join us. Even the chancellor was impressed by the latest. Tell him that when he's back.'

They were discussing the latest report. Gareth was in Washington, talking to the CIA. The latest Timber Wolf report had been shown to the prime minister but for the time being was withheld from the negotiating team in Brussels in case through their manner they betrayed nonchalance about the EU's public position. Charles was privately relieved that Gareth wasn't around to fuel the enthusiasm. 'Nonetheless, we shouldn't regard that figure in the report as set in stone,' he cautioned. 'They might change their minds about it.'

Robin's disarmingly boyish features briefly creased with concern. 'But the sub-sources are sound, aren't they? Authoritative? Horse's mouth stuff?'

'Very much so, yes.'

'And you trust Gareth to get it right, of course?'

Robin's appearance of youthful innocence concealed a mind that gripped like a bear-trap. He and Gareth had served together in New York and Charles had the impression of mutual wariness, each ever watchful for chinks in the other's armour. Charles chose his words carefully. 'I'm confident Gareth knows exactly what he's saying. He wouldn't just get it wrong.'

'But you are sure that what he says is right?'

'As sure as I can be. So is he. It's just that I'm cautioning against the assumption that the EU wouldn't ever change their minds about what their bottom line is. Just as we do, now and again.' He disliked temporising but to do otherwise would risk undermining the whole stream of Timber Wolf reporting, perhaps unfairly.

'The foreign secretary would like a chat with Gareth when he's back.' Robin folded his napkin. 'You see him as your successor?'

It was another indication that others saw him as becoming the past. 'A strong contender, certainly.'

'Just make sure you stick around long enough so that no one can argue that we should advertise the post to EU nationals.'

Gareth would be away for another three days. Charles described the case to Sarah over dinner that night, without revealing Timber Wolf's identity. He trusted her discretion and, being outside the Office but familiar with it, her perspective was useful. Also, she knew Gareth. Her verdict was swift and succinct.

'You must have it out with Gareth before he sees Timber Wolf again. You must be absolutely straight with him that the meetings must be recorded except that, assuming you want to keep Sonia out of it, you say you're doing it under pressure from Whitehall. You've given them cast-iron guarantees about Timber Wolf's reports and in so doing you've put your own head on the line. You want to be able to tell them that he's been recorded word for word and you're satisfied he's pukka. Gareth can't reasonably resist a covert recording and if he does you have your answer, don't you? At least, you're halfway to it. Also, if I were you I'd be more concerned to please Sonia, given her record and what she did for you, than to avoid offending Gareth. You know what I feel about him. Slimy toad. I hated that weekend we spent with them in Carcassonne, every minute of it. The way he treated Suzanne was so embarrassing, the way he spoke to her, I mean. I couldn't understand how you've been such good friends with him for so long. It's different between men, I suppose. I wouldn't trust him an inch.'

Charles was well aware of her feelings about Gareth. 'He's good at his job, always has been.'

'Maybe that says something about the job.' She smiled and put her hand on his arm. 'I don't mean that. Well, only half. I'm sure you're good at it too and you're not like Gareth. So far as I know.'

Charles wasn't so sure. He had always felt that he and Gareth had quite a lot in common, at least in the professional sphere. Their assumptions, judgements and instincts were usually close enough to dispense with explanation, itself suggestive of some deeper commonality that he preferred to leave unexamined, for the time being at least.

Sarah smiled again. 'Anyway, it's my turn now. I have

a dinner agenda item too.' She had that day spent thirty minutes with an MI5 desk officer as a result of Michael Dunton's request to Charles. 'At desk level MI5 seem more worried about Daniel than Michael suggested to you. She – the woman who came to see me – said he's left the mosque near where they live and has joined a small breakaway one, every member of which has at some time or other been suspected of plotting or aspiring to do something awful. One of them is a Guantanamo graduate, picked up in Afghanistan doing alleged charity work, apparently, and released a couple of years ago. Since when they believe he's re-engaged with his dodgy charity work. They don't have a mosque as such; they meet in each other's houses or flats, about half a dozen of them. They have a self-appointed imam who has already served time under the Prevention of Terrorism Act on a conspiracy charge. The police wanted to get him for something more serious but that would have meant a lot more surveillance at a time when resources were very stretched and they didn't want to risk him committing some awful atrocity that they missed. So they went for disruption.

'Well, it now appears that the imam and my beloved godson are pretty thick with each other and she wanted to know whether I thought Daniel was recruitable as a source on the rest of the group. None of the others is remotely recruitable, apparently. I rather got the impression she'd like us to recruit him for them, though she didn't actually say so in so many words. I said this was all much more your sort of judgement than mine and I'd talk to you about it, since you know him too. I also said we'd try to get the happy couple round for dinner soon, which we ought to do anyway. Then you can write a report for MI5. I said you'd be very happy to do that. So, diaries, dates.' She was smiling as she took her phone from her handbag, then took Charles's pocket diary from the drawer where he kept his wallet and credit cards and put it on the table before him. 'When will you get round to using electronic diaries? You must drive them mad in your office.'

'First thing that happens when I get in in the morning is that Jenny grabs my diary and puts any new entries on screen. So both diaries are always up to date. Much more reliable than trusting me to do it.'

'But why use a paper diary at all when you've got your phone and laptop? Such a duplication of effort.'

'I like my diary.'

'You just like being awkward and getting attention.'

Gareth's absence meant there was time for another session with Sonia before Charles confronted him. Not wanting to give the impression even to his private office that there was anything untoward, he arranged another out-of-office briefing, this time over an evening pizza at home in Cowley Street.

'Since Swinbrook I've been through all the Timber Wolf write-ups again,' said Sonia. 'I've also asked Cheltenham for a printout of his cyber footprint. As with all of us, it's much bigger and more densely populated than you'd think. Gets around, does our Timber Wolf.

'Aged forty-seven, born in s'Hertogenbosch, father a lawyer, mother a teacher, educated locally, then at university in Nijmegen where he read law. Then he somehow got a place at ENA, you know, the French academy for administrators through which the entire French elite perpetuates itself. Then the Dutch foreign service and Geneva where he met Gareth, also a number of other of our people and the Foreign Office's. Next he's posted to Brussels as part of the Dutch mission to the EU, then he resigns and joins the EU itself. His Brussels contacts are many, as you might imagine, but interestingly they don't appear to include any of the current EU negotiating team who are so regularly indiscreet with him, according to Gareth.'

'Maybe because he works alongside them every day so doesn't need to communicate outside the office.'

'Maybe. By his own account, he advises the negotiating team on ensuring that proposals emerging from the negotiating process are legally compatible with wider EU policy, particularly ever-closer union. But his office is not on the same floor as theirs. In fact, he's on the same floor as the president. His official job description – which seems to have emerged only about a year ago – is Advisor to the President on Policy Coherence. Which means everything and nothing, of course.'

'No indication how much time he spends with the negotiating team, visits their offices, socialises with them or whatever?'

'None. His wife is Belgian, a former ballerina who teaches dance. Most of their socialising seems to focus around her friends, a fairly arty crowd. He belongs to an EU gym, exercises regularly, takes the boys skating on the Dutch canals in winter. They're seventeen and fourteen, both at school in Brussels. A pretty comfortable, well-balanced life on the whole, well paid, very low taxes as an EU official, very generous pension. Most other travel is in the course of his work.'

'Where?'

'Paris, Berlin, Warsaw, Washington, Beijing, London. Or used to. He hasn't travelled since the referendum except here, when he met Gareth.' She picked up a piece of pizza crust from the side of her plate, broke off the end and chewed it slowly. 'All their meetings since then have been in Brussels, all in suitably expensive restaurants and hotels.'

'What's Gareth's cover for being there?'

'Liaising with the British mission to the EU, plus a bit of catching up with old friends.'

'Timber Wolf being the only one?'

'Not quite.' She sipped her wine. 'I wasn't sure whether to tell you since it's personal and probably unconnected with the case.'

'A woman.'

'Naturally. A French official, Monique something, forty-one, unmarried, part of the French mission to the EU. They too met in Geneva. She's part of Timber Wolf's cyber footprint because they also knew each other in Geneva and they still have occasional dealings, more official than Gareth's sort. He pops up as being a contact of both of them.'

'And he's having an affair with her?'

'Probably, knowing Gareth. It's not absolutely clear, though it would doubtless be easy enough to find out if you were to do a proper job on both of them.'

Charles didn't want to think about that. 'So what do you conclude about Gareth and Timber Wolf?'

'That they meet as and when he says they do, that they must talk about something, that it's possible that Timber Wolf talks as Gareth says and also possible that Gareth consciously or unconsciously exaggerates or puts words into Timber Wolf's mouth.'

'And you think he does?'

She looked at him for a while, then sighed. 'I think it's more likely that he is exaggerating than that Timber Wolf is saying exactly what Gareth says he says. Partly for the reasons I gave in Swinbrook and partly because it's too good to be true, all this bottom line stuff. I just don't see why Timber Wolf should suddenly start doing it. He's got nothing to gain, he's hitherto been an evangelist for the EU project, for a USE, United States of Europe, and so far as I can see he doesn't talk to anyone else in this way. I suspect Gareth not so much of fabricating as of embroidering, perhaps embroidering hugely, thereby hugely enhancing his own career, as he hopes. And at the same time providing excellent cover for seeing his mistress. Note that none of his trips are day trips, which they easily could be. He always stays a night, sometimes two.'

'And what about expenses?' asked Charles. 'Is Timber Wolf taking money and, if so, for what? By your account, he can't have any real expenses beyond perhaps the odd cab fare to the restaurant. Which he wouldn't notice anyway on his salary. Gareth pays for their meals but his claims are way over what even the most exorbitant Brussels lunches cost. So where is that money going? Either Gareth's on the fiddle, which I find hard to believe – he doesn't need the money – or it's going to Timber Wolf in undeclared payments for product. In which case, why not declare it?'

Sonia sat back, smoothing her short hair with both hands. 'That's for you to sort out, isn't it, I'm happy to say. You're the boss.'

Chapter Five

'They're not vegetarian, are they?' Sarah asked while they were still in bed the day before Daniel and his wife, Akela, were due for dinner.

'Probably.'

That evening she said, 'Daniel aspires to be vegetarian but isn't very strict. Akela, on the other hand, is the real deal. Deborah says that Daniel started out being strict but when he gave up alcohol he became an occasional carnivore again. We must get used to calling him Abdul.'

'Must we?'

'You'd expect your family to make an effort, wouldn't you, if you'd changed your name?'

'Not my family.'

Charles had suggested they took them out for dinner but Sarah felt that would look too much as if they didn't want to be bothered with cooking at home, which was true. 'Besides, I feel I ought to make some effort for my godson.'

'For Deborah, you mean.'

When the day came Akela arrived in a black trouser suit and white blouse, though she still wore her headscarf. Daniel wore clean jeans and a lurid green jersey. 'Do we call you Daniel or Abdul?' Charles asked as he invited them in. 'We want to get it right.'

Daniel smiled. 'Whichever is easier for you. My friends and Akela's family call me Abdul but my family and people who've known me all my life can be forgiven for calling me Daniel. The Prophet – peace and blessings be upon Him – is tolerant of other beliefs.'

Reluctant either to contradict any form of religious avowal or to allow his endorsement to be tacitly assumed, Charles's usual response was a swift transfer to another topic. This time, though, he felt he should make the effort to engage.

'I believe Islam had an early reputation for tolerance of other faiths, didn't it? With religions of the Book, anyway.'

'The Muslims permitted Jews and Christians to live among them while keeping alive the flame of learning during what Christians call the Dark Ages. Many Jews and Christians, perceiving truth, converted. You will hear some people argue that there were forced conversions and that those who refused suffered discrimination, but that is part of Christianity's anti-Muslim mythology.'

Daniel had stepped through the door first and now he stopped as he spoke, keeping Akela behind him in the narrow hall. 'We're lucky to live in a time of religious toleration,' Charles said as he tried to usher them through.

Daniel ignored or failed to notice the gesture. He folded one arm, rested the other elbow on it and stood stroking his soft red beard. 'From the days of its birth Islam has had to struggle against those who seek to suppress the truth. In 1095 Pope Urban II launched the Crusades that began with Christian slaughtering of the Jews in Europe. Four years later the crusading Christians murdered 70,000 men, women and children in Jerusalem. They boiled Muslims in cooking pots and roasted children on spits. But when the Muslims under Saladin recaptured Jerusalem in 1187 they spared the Christians and protected the holy places. Yet to this day Christians continue to depict Islam as a threat and Muslims as barbaric and inferior.'

Akela squeezed past her husband with a submissive smile and went through to Sarah in the kitchen. 'D'you think they do?' Charles adopted what he hoped was a tone of disinterested scholarly enquiry while again indicating to Daniel that they should move into the sitting room. 'Most of those I've met—'

'During the colonial period the Christian west plundered and looted Muslim countries and when oil was discovered they dismembered the Ottoman Empire, destroyed the Caliphate and used the infamous

Sykes–Picot agreement to enable the Zionist land-grab in which powers that did not own the Holy Lands of Palestine gave them to the Zionist jackal that has suppressed and terrorised the Palestinians ever since and which they support to this day.'

'What can I get you to drink?' Charles stepped decisively into the sitting room, leaving Daniel to follow. In recent years he had become all too familiar with the Single Narrative, the centuries-old litany of Muslim victimhood comprising truths, half-truths, fictions and myths. 'Fortunately, Muslim integration into British society is working quite well, isn't it? Compared with other countries. You and Akela, for example—'

'Islam is politics and society or it is nothing. Islam cannot be integrated without ceasing to be Islam. It is necessary for it to become the society it inhabits. Some Muslims argue that we should participate in elections in order to bring the Islamic movement to power so that the necessary changes can then be made. But others argue that the democratic path is a Western illusion, that it has failed Muslims in Algeria, Jordan, Egypt and Palestine and that anyway it violates the sharia. For myself—'

'Elderflower cordial?'

'Thank you.'

'And for Akela?'

'She drinks only water.'

Daniel remained in the middle of the room, holding

forth. Charles let him run on in the hope that a sermon before dinner would prevent a sermon during it. During the ensuing ten minutes they covered the 1953 removal by Britain and America of the popular Iranian government and the installation of the Shah, and then Suez, before reverting to the 1948 founding of Israel by Western powers anxious to assuage their guilt over Christian and fascist responsibility for what they called the Holocaust, which they continued to exaggerate in order to justify the usurper Israel. They also touched on Western responsibility for Iraq and Syria, Western indifference to the massacres of Muslims in Bosnia and Chechnya, Western tolerance of pornography and of vile mocking films and cartoons of the Prophet in Denmark and Holland and of the persecution of innocent Muslims under iniquitous counter-terrorism legislation introduced since 9/11.

Charles, having listened in silence, thought he may as well go the whole hog and confirm what he suspected. 'Yes, 9/11.' He shook his head. 'Who do you think was responsible?'

Daniel was holding his glass in both hands now, as if it were an offering. 'The Jews and the CIA.'

They searched each other's eyes for a moment, Charles for any flicker of irony and Daniel, he suspected, for signs of hostility and resistance. 'More elderflower?'

*

Dinner was easier than the preliminaries had threatened. Akela was quiet, answering questions but initiating nothing. She was a civil servant in the Department for Education and looked forward to leaving when they started a family, which she spoke of as a foregone conclusion. She ate little of the vegetarian lasagne that Sarah had spent the previous evening preparing. It was hard to imagine that she and her ebullient lawyer sister had much in common.

Daniel, having got his ideology off his chest, proved happy to engage on subjects other than the Single Narrative. They discussed his carpentering and the pleasures and pains of self-employment in southwest London. Once or twice he veered back towards the ideological but Charles was able to distract him from a full sermon by generalising about the Single Narratives of other cultures and countries, such as the Russian version of the Second World War and the Cold War, the Irish Republican passion for grievance and the benign history of the British Empire that he had grown up with.

Afterwards, when he and Sarah were clearing up, he told her of another obsessive he had known, an older man, a dentist, sensitive and artistic, who had been among the first troops into the Belsen concentration camp in 1945. In later life he had made beautiful, suffering miniature figures from his dental materials while becoming obsessed by the world's population increase. This concern found a way into every conversation until eventually it became impossible to talk to him about anything else. When he killed himself – also using dental materials – he left a note saying he had done it to reduce the world's population. Charles recalled his own unfeeling youthful reflection that, if that really was his concern, it might have been more rational to murder his daughters.

'But Daniel's not as monomaniacal as that,' said Sarah. 'He was talking quite normally for most of dinner. Anyway, he seems too keen on it all to kill himself– it's a sin in Islam as in Christianity, isn't it? Unless you seek martyrdom in battle while defending the cause.'

'He thinks terrorists are martyrs.'

'But that's almost conventional, isn't it?'

'Among extremists.'

'He doesn't seem that extreme to me, no more than Christians who believe in creation myths or transubstantiation. I don't get the impression he's going to set about non-believers with his hammer and chisel, do you?'

'Except that what he espouses amounts to a call to action rather than a statement of faith.'

'It's just the enthusiasm of the convert, if you ask me.'

'Obsessives are wearisome, all of them. They're not all mad but I think he's going that way.'

'I don't. I think he knows a hawk from a handsaw.'

'Do you?'

He arranged the session with Gareth for seven the following evening, not late enough to be out of the ordinary but a time by which most people would have gone home. They would be alone. He had told his secretary – he still thought of her as that rather than as his EA, executive assistant, as secretaries were now styled – to tell Gareth's EA that it was to discuss a development strategy for Timber Wolf reporting. Gareth liked discussing such concepts and would not, Charles hoped, arrive in defensive mode.

Much of the afternoon was taken up with meetings and repetitive discussions about the Operation Tresco submission. Tresco was an operation against the Islamic State group in Syria aimed at identifying and, where legally permissible, capturing or killing senior leaders and any others thought to pose a threat to the UK. The main penetration agent, a British-based Afghan codenamed Herm, had got alongside a major target, Tresco/1, a Birmingham-born Briton of Pakistani origin who had joined al-Qaeda before transferring to IS, where he now trained others like himself to return to the UK and kill people. As well as training those on the ground, he provided Internet coaching to so-called lone wolves resident within the UK. One had recently driven a car into a group of Liverpool football supporters, killing one and injuring three. He was armed with two knives and had been arrested at the scene by police using tasers. Meanwhile, in Syria Herm had made contact with Tresco/1 at the flaying and execution of suspected spies. Herm's knowledge of Britain led to his being instructed to help with training. The aim of the operation was for Herm to plant a guidance device on Tresco/1 that could be used in a drone attack.

Submissions that could lead to a killing had to be approved by the prime minister and the to-ing and fro-ing of the afternoon between MI6 legal advisors, Foreign Office legal advisors, Number Ten and the MOD had concerned whether the wording required for legal conformity properly matched the facts as known. During moments when he was alone with his screen Charles would turn away and gaze out of his window towards the Embankment and the Thames, finding that in the opacity of the stretch of water he could glimpse something that lifted his thoughts from the immediate. That had been the essence of his passion for fishing when he was a boy; not so much the fish he caught as the solitude and mystery of being by water, the lure of the unseen. Now, musing on what they were doing, he wondered whether he lacked moral concern. Everyone else involved in the Tresco submission seemed morally satisfied, their concern being to demonstrate legal conformity rather than ethical rightness. Anyone with qualms could ask to be assigned to other work, or transfer out. Not that the killing of a killer troubled Charles. He had done it himself. Doing it remotely via a drone seemed morally no different from killing with a sniper rifle, which in the case of Tresco/1 he would have been happy to do.

What concerned him was the lack of thought given to Herm, whom he and Gareth had recruited many years ago. Herm was then a medical student in London, an Afghan refugee whose residency status was unclear even to the Home Office. He had been interviewed by MI5 about a terrorist he was thought to know and, as he had run out of money and was about to give up his training and return to Afghanistan, he had been passed to MI6 as a possible useful contact. Charles, then London-based, had been asked to assess him. He found a stocky, serious-minded, seemingly fearless young man who hated al-Qaeda and the Taliban for the damage they had wrought upon his country and was prepared to work against them. Charles persuaded him he should finish his training, discreetly funded by MI6 on the understanding that he would remain in contact when he returned to Afghanistan. Before he left Charles handed him over to Gareth, who was about to join the Kabul station. Gareth handled him well and during his Kabul tour turned Herm into a useful source on extremists he came across through his wide-ranging medical practice.

Charles had then lost sight of the case until recently learning that Herm was still on the books as a doctor in IS-occupied Syria, co-operating with IS for the sake of his patients but secretly reporting via a young case officer who crossed the border from Iraq for clandestine meetings under Special Forces protection. Tresco/1 had come to Herm as a patient with a slight shrapnel wound. Finding that his doctor knew London, he had sought his advice on key points and bomb targets. Herm had obliged and reported back. After witnessing Tresco/1 executing two teenage Syrian boys, supposed spies, and a French journalist, he had offered to plant a homing device so that Tresco/1 could be killed. Tresco/1 changed his mobile phone frequently, but it was always the same kind and from the same supplier. Herm was provided with an identical doctored handset, which he was to substitute for Tesco/1's latest when occasion arose.

It was Herm himself whom Charles pondered now: how old would he be, had he married and had a family, would he ever settle, were medicine and spying the twin poles of his existence, did he do it for love or duty, how long might he last when at any moment an IS extremist might suspect him or a Russian bomb might haphazardly fall close? The Office was presumably paying him or putting money aside and would resettle him if he survived, but was that enough for what he was doing, the risks he was taking? For everyone else on that email chain, from Downing Street downwards, it was a job; they went home every night. But for Herm, as for every spy, there was no such thing as down time, no such thing as time off. Spying was his life and might easily become his death. Every minute he lived through, waking or sleeping, was spent under threat of exposure.

Charles was still gazing towards the river when Gareth arrived, fashionably tie-less, his suit jacket slung over his shoulder. 'Bloody JIC,' he said. 'Have you seen what the next paper's to be? A report on international adherence to climate change objectives, the idea being that we find out who's cheating by supplying made-up figures so that we can put diplomatic pressure on them to reform. Soft power gets softer by the day.'

Charles stood and indicated the armchairs by the coffee table. 'Drink of something?'

'Whisky, I need a whisky. Splash of water, no ice.'

Charles poured himself the same from his drinks drawer and took the other chair. They talked about the JIC – Joint Intelligence Committee – for a while, speculating about its survival now that the National Security Committee had usurped an important part of its function. The latter was chaired by the prime minister or other senior ministers and so Charles and the other heads of agencies naturally attended that, delegating the JIC, which they had formerly attended, to their deputies.

'The problem with the JIC is its passion for consensus,' said Gareth. 'Always has been. Makes their reports so bland they're like – well, like water without whisky. Not that I'm accusing you of being stingy.'

They both smiled. 'Timber Wolf,' said Charles. 'This seems a good time to map out where we're going. Where we hope to go.'

'I heard this afternoon that his latest has gone down very well, especially in Number Ten. The Brexiteers are gagging for more.'

'And in order to work out where we're going we need to be sure about where we are.' It was a shot across the bows. Gareth nodded, with a slight tightening of the flesh around his mouth. Charles tried to sound as if he were thinking aloud. 'First thing we need to get straight – I need to get straight, in my own mind – are his sub-sources. Who are they, exactly?'

'Well, basically the negotiating team.'

'All of them? How many are there?'

'Depends how you define it. They're not all at the table. There are quite a few backroom people.'

'But which of them tell him things?' Charles reached for the notepad and pencil he had placed on the table in advance.

Gareth shrugged, as if this were a minor matter. 'Not sure I can remember offhand but I'll have a go.'

He paused, then listed three names, which Charles noted. Two were familiar to him from Foreign Office reporting. It was worrying that Gareth should struggle to remember. The Gareth of their youth, his fellow case officer, would have had all his agents' sub-sources off pat. 'Any idea what their responsibilities are?'

'Not without looking them up.'

Charles put down his pencil, picked up his whisky and sat back, as if relaxing. 'Why do you think he talks to you? What's his motivation?'

Gareth also sat back. 'Good question. I'm not sure I really know. Friendship is part of it, I guess. Must be. We've known each other a long time. He trusts me.'

'But he must realise you're reporting it, given that he knows what you do?'

'Trusts me not to let him down. Knows I'll protect his identity. And I think he genuinely wants an amicable Brexit. He's quite an Anglophile, like a lot of Dutch. Wants both sides to win. He probably sees giving me their fallback position as helping us all to a reasonable compromise. I'm sure there are plenty of Foreign Office Remainers who would do the same if the boot were on the other foot.'

'He's taking a hell of a risk – his job and Brussels are his life – for nothing in return.'

'Not quite nothing. He gets the best meals in Brussels, better than any he'd get in Paris.'

'And his expenses.'

'Christ, yes. He likes his expenses, does Timber Wolf.'

'What for?'

'What?'

'What are his expenses for?'

Gareth turned his head towards the long-case clock, as if to read the answer in its face. It was the Cumming clock, made by the first chief of MI6, probably from materials scrounged from naval dockyards. Charles had had it rescued from the lumber room to which his predecessor had confined it. Gareth looked back with the grin of a sheepish schoolboy. 'Okay, fair cop, guv. He doesn't really have any expenses, of course. It's effectively a payment, which he knows very well and finds very acceptable so long as he's not confronted with the unpalatable fact that he's being paid for intelligence. I've called it expenses from the moment I offered it.'

'No mention of this on file.'

Gareth held up his hands. 'Fair cop again. If I had it would have become an agent case, which would have needed clearance from the Foreign Office, Number Ten and God Almighty. Imagine it: a submission to recruit, pay and run an EU official during the most sensitive negotiations we're ever likely to conduct. And imagine the political fallout if it ever came out. It wouldn't have stood a cat in hell's chance, no point in even asking. So I reckoned that so long as I kept up the expenses fiction, claiming as if for myself and pretending it was just two old friends getting together for a routine diplomatic exchange, it wouldn't put Timber Wolf, you or HMG in a fantastically difficult position. Less said the better, in other words. Wouldn't be the first time you and I have played that one, would it?'

This time it was Charles who paused. Maintaining such a fiction with an agent who wouldn't want to be confronted with the truth was one thing, but keeping it from the Office was quite another. Gareth was right that the need for clearance could sometimes be navigated around, but not in this case, nor on this subject. For some seconds the dignified ticking of Cumming's clock filled the room. It was a clock that ran true. 'We must go for clearance, retrospective clearance,' he said. 'We must have the prime minister and foreign secretary signed up for it. Otherwise it's not just my head on the line, it's the Service itself.'

'Well, that's the end of the case. They'll never agree. Why not carry on as we are? If no one's confronted with what we're doing, no harm done. Timber Wolf's happy to chat, we're happy to listen, Whitehall's happy to read the product. Everybody's happy, just so long as it's not spelt out. Spying – successful spying – makes the world a happier place for everyone. You've said it yourself.' Gareth was smiling again now but there was a petulant edge to his voice.

In his own operational career Charles, like Gareth,

had taken risks, occasionally physical but more often bureaucratic, choosing to economise with the truth until the time was right for disclosure. But now he meant what he said about the risk to the Service, possibly a terminal risk. He didn't mind being the MI6 chief who was sacked but he didn't want to be the last chief. Every government needed a security service, an MI5, in some form, even as part of the police, but by no means every government needed or had a secret service. That depended on having a forward foreign policy, a perception that the national interest needed protecting and advancing. After years of emasculation, that was no longer an automatic assumption. 'Sorry, Gareth, but we must go for it. It will mean coming clean about what's going on. When's your next meeting with Timber Wolf?'

'Sixth of next month.'

'That should give us time. I'll talk to Robin Woodstock before going into print. He might give a helpful steer if the shock doesn't kill him. Meanwhile, no contact with Timber Wolf until we've sorted this out.'

'Fair enough.'

Gareth stood. Charles had not expected him to concede so easily. He stood too.

'Tell me something,' said Gareth. 'Is Sonia behind this?'

'No.'

There was another pause as they faced each other, then Gareth put down his empty glass and walked out.

Charles remained as he was for a moment or two then, still holding his untouched whisky, returned to his desk and reached for his phone. It rang before he picked it up.

'Oh, you are still there. Thank goodness I've got you,' said Sarah. 'I'm still here – at work – too but I've just had a call from Anya, Akela's sister, remember? She wants to come and see us this evening. It concerns Daniel but she didn't want to talk about it on the phone. I told her I'd be back by about eight-thirty but now I'm not sure I'll be on time. Will you be back by then?'

'I can be.'

'Have you done that note for Michael Dunton's MI5 desk officer?'

'Not yet.'

'Sounds as if there might be more to add.'

Before he left Charles emailed Robin Woodstock in the Foreign Office requesting a meeting the following morning. As he walked home across Smith Square, where concertgoers were crowding on the steps of St John's, his mind was not so much on the clearance he believed they would never get as on Gareth's account of Timber Wolf's motives. Agents who were indiscreet because of friendship, trust and goodwill were generally not venal, unlikely to accept unquestioned money for expenses they knew they hadn't incurred. And, generous though the expenses were, they were nothing to what Timber Wolf earned.

As soon as he was in the house he rang Sonia, asking her to come in early the following morning so that he could try out a theory on her. The call was cut short by a single, tentative knock on the door. It was Anya. Sarah arrived by taxi just as he was showing her in and there were a few minutes of flustered half-sentences as Anya gushed apologies and Sarah gushed reassurances. They sat at the kitchen table and Charles opened a bottle of French dry white. Sarah asked Anya about her job, which led to a discussion about the merits and demerits of law as a profession, of City firms in particular and of the changes in legal training that Anya was now undergoing. Finding his glass nearly empty and embarrassed to pour another while the others had barely sipped theirs, Charles interrupted. 'What was it you wanted to talk about?'

Anya ceased smiling and took a long sip at her own wine. 'I am worried about my sister and Abdul – Daniel. They had a very nice dinner here with you, I know. I heard from her and she enjoyed it very much. And she and Abdul are very happy together. They love each other, I am sure. But – it feels disloyal to say this but I don't know who else I can say it to and

I don't want to get Daniel into trouble with the police for something that may be quite innocent. I hope you can, in your position, stop that happening, Mr Thoroughgood?'

Charles now poured himself more wine. 'I have no executive authority. I can't interfere if a crime has been committed. Indeed, I have an obligation to report it, as any other citizen has. That said, I'll happily advise or help in any way I can. But I need to know what we're talking about.'

Sarah got some cheese biscuits and crisps from the cupboard and poured them into glass bowls.

Anya nodded. 'I'm worried that Abdul has too much – too much Islam, if you see what I mean. My family is very moderate, which is traditional for the part of India we come from. My parents, that is. We believe, of course, and we go to the mosque – my parents, anyway – and we keep the festivals, Eid and such things. But we are not extreme, not in any way. We drink'– she smiled as she raised her glass – 'and we live basically a Western life. As you can see from me. Though I am the least observant of all my family, much less than Akela. And even she is not extreme, not at all, just conservative. But Abdul – Daniel – he is ... he has left our mosque and started going to another, a small mosque with a big reputation. Not a good reputation. I don't even know where it is but I have heard about it. He is becoming more devout than any of us and I am worried that he is being influenced by extremists. He spends a lot of time looking at websites, Akela tells me, and now he has forbidden music in their house. He says it is un-Islamic, which is nonsense but it's what some extremists say. He threw out all their CDs and he wants Akela to wear the burka but she won't, not while she's working, anyway. Excuse me.'

She broke off to blow her nose, then sipped more of her wine and helped herself to a single small cheese biscuit. 'One is never enough,' said Charles, pushing the bowl towards her.

She took another. 'And now he has done something else, I hear from Akela. He went out and bought some knives, big ones with long blades like carving knives.'

'Do vegetarians use carving knives?' asked Sarah. 'Perhaps they do. But definitely a domestic knife rather than a hunting knife or commando knife or whatever they're called?'

'I think so, yes. Akela is very worried because of all these knife attacks by extremists. She doesn't believe Abdul is an extremist but she knows he looks at all those websites and he is becoming more and more strict with her, even since their marriage. She hasn't told my parents any of this. They just think Abdul's enthusiasm is the normal enthusiasm of the convert and that he will moderate in time.'

'Could it be that he thought they simply needed some knives?' asked Sarah.

'Of course but Akela didn't think so and hadn't said so to him.'

'Has she asked him why he got them?'

'No. She doesn't like to. I think she's frightened.' She looked at Charles. 'As I said, I don't want to get them into trouble, to get Abdul arrested or anything. It may all be quite innocent. Please God it is. Can you do anything?'

'I can pass it on to the people who study terrorism and see what they think but I don't have to report it to the police unless he's actually done something illegal, which it doesn't sound as if he has.' His reassurance was misleading, while being literally true. Reporting it to MI5 would mean it would go onto Daniel's electronic file, as he was already a subject of interest. If he moved higher up the target ladder or said or did anything to bring himself to attention, it would automatically be shared with SO15, the Metropolitan Police counter-terrorism branch. 'Meanwhile, keep talking to Akela, get her to tell you anything that worries her no matter how trivial and let us know, either of us. The more we know the easier it is to reach a balanced judgement and to assess whether there's really anything to worry about or whether it's just the enthusiasm of the convert, as you suggested. But thank you for telling us. You did exactly the right thing and we'll keep an eye on it together.'

'Stay for dinner,' said Sarah. 'There's masses in the freezer.'

She declined, leaving when she'd finished her wine and after more talk about her future with her law firm. Her training contract was coming to an end and she didn't know whether she was going to be offered a position. She would go back to the office now, though it would be nearly ten by the time she got there.

'Keep in touch about the job too,' said Sarah. 'I mentor trainees so I hear what's going on in our firm and elsewhere.'

Over defrosted salmon they watched television news coverage of the knife attack in Ely cathedral in which three visitors and a guide were injured, the guide later dying of her wounds. The attacker, a man described as of Middle Eastern appearance, fled into the town. Police were searching streets and gardens and making house-to-house calls in case a family was being held hostage. Residents were advised to stay inside. A Home Office minister said that the government was keeping an open mind on whether it was a terrorist act.

'Every time we hear something like this now I'm going to worry that it's Daniel,' said Sarah. 'Poor Deborah. I hope she's got no inkling of what Anya was saying.'

'Chances are Daniel's not going that way.'

'How can you be so sure?'

'I'm not. I just think it's unlikely. He seems too open about it, too pleased to show off his new faith to be secretly plotting murder and mayhem. Granted, anyone's capable of anything, depending on context, but it's unlikely in his case. Mad, maybe, but not bad. Anyway, most things never happen, as Philip Larkin tells us.'

'You really think anyone's capable of anything?'

'More or less, depending on context.'

'I'm not sure which is worse, Islamist extremism or having Philip Larkin as your lord and guide.'

After the news Sarah went up to work in the third bedroom, which they had turned into a study, while Charles sat at the kitchen table with his laptop and red box. The box had been delivered by car that evening, filled with papers in addition to those on the secure laptop. For anything requiring sustained concentration he preferred to work from paper. It was, he acknowledged, another sign of generational redundancy; younger people would simply never know the advantage of paper.

However, he wrote his note on Daniel for MI5 on-screen, having already got the desk officer's designation from Michael Dunton but copying it to Michael anyway. He mentioned the knife purchase, adding that in the time he had known Daniel he had seen nothing to indicate a propensity to violence in him. Then with a heavy heart he lifted from the red box the inch-thick paper on resources and the forthcoming showdown with the Treasury, the most consequential issue he was currently involved with. There was a meeting about it the following morning after his hoped-for Foreign Office meeting with Robin Woodstock. Finances were a mess, barely comprehensible as well as in short supply. He hated having to attend to them, acknowledging to himself that this was not the mark of a great – or perhaps even adequate – chief. Nevertheless, he would be expected to have a good grasp, with clear and well-argued reasons why they should have more, or at least not have less. It would not be a good morning.

Chapter Six

He met Sonia early the next morning in the Regency Cafe, ten minutes' walk from Smith Square, just off Horseferry Road. His excuse for meeting her there, knowing she wouldn't like it, was that they were unlikely to meet anyone from the Office. He liked the place for its thick uncompromising mugs of tea or coffee, its generous fried breakfasts, its gruff but well-mannered working clientele and for the man and woman who called out the orders in parade-ground voices. The noise was such that there was no danger of being overheard. He was the only suit there.

She hunched over her tea, glancing furtively at the exclusively male customers. 'How can they eat all that? I don't think they'd heard of mint tea when I asked for it. And this is so strong I can almost stand my spoon in it.' She winced as the woman bellowed out an order for two-fried-eggs-fried-bread-bacon-beans-fried-potato-mushrooms-tomatos-two-teas. She nodded at Charles's plate. 'I don't know how you can eat all that.'

'I like to have something to look forward to when I get up. The rest of the day could be pretty bleak. At least there's no music here.'

'No one would hear it. You wouldn't bring Sarah here, would you?'

'She wouldn't come.'

'Anyway, how did Gareth take your news?'

'Not well.' He described the interview. 'My worry is that if he's making it up – possible but unlikely – how are we going to tell the Foreign Office and Whitehall that the intelligence they've been relying on and which they say is making a difference to the negotiations is a fantasy, made up by the case officer? They'd close us down.'

'Your head would be on the block, that's for sure. Mind you, it's been there before and you haven't yet been parted from it.'

'My head's the least of it. In fact, I don't think he can be making it up. Not all of it, anyway. More likely he's exaggerating and embroidering, as we suspect, rather than inventing. And doing a very good job of it. When he's predicted they'll say X or Y in negotiations it's turned out to be true, give or take a bit. He couldn't invent that sort of stuff without the gift of prophecy. He's been right too often to be right by chance.'

'But would inventing really be that difficult for anyone who follows what's going on? The big themes are all predictable – you don't need secret intelligence to identify what's going to come across the table at you, the major concerns of both sides are signalled in advance. You could probably invent plausibly so long as you don't go into too much detail.'

'But Whitehall likes it and they're the experts.'

'Only because it conforms to what they already know or suspect. Has any of Timber Wolf's reporting – alleged reporting – been truly game-changing? Or even surprising?' She screwed up her face again at another bellowed order.

'Maybe that's the nature of these negotiations, with so much played out in public beforehand as leaks or press speculation. What persuades me that some at least of it is real is the similarity of phrasing between Timber Wolf's predictions and the write-ups we see of the negotiations. If you do a textual analysis there's clearly a common source.'

'But you say he's still shifty about Timber Wolf's sub-sources. Why should that be? Why should he be reluctant to name them? I'm sure he always has in the past, with any other case he's done.'

Charles nodded. 'The only reason I can think of is the most unpalatable one – there aren't any.' He finished his tea. 'Thing is, what am I going to say to Robin Woodstock in the Foreign Office in fifty minutes? I don't want them to go off the deep end and mistrust all Timber Wolf reporting – which, with a handful of other cases elsewhere, is what our reputation in Whitehall rests on at the moment – but nor do I want to have to creep along subsequently when it all blows up in our faces and confess that we've been worried about this for a while but didn't like to say so. As spies, we are midwives to truth. We have to be, that's our mission. We deceive to reveal. Our obligation is to deliver, however unpalatable.'

'I really can't manage any more of this.' She pushed her tea aside. 'Do you have to say anything yet? Why not wait until you have a full story to tell that you know to be true rather than half a story and a raft of unverified suspicions? After all, what can Robin do with half a story – react, not react, wait and see? By sharing it you're simply foisting our uncertainty on him, as if you're absolving us of sole responsibility. Of course, I know I'm playing devil's advocate here, having raised the doubts myself.' She smiled. 'I think you should say as little as you can and meanwhile we investigate.'

'How?'

'You've forbidden Gareth any more Timber Wolf meetings?'

'For the time being.'

'Someone else should see Timber Wolf.'

'You?' He could imagine the effect on Gareth. But

Sonia would get to the bottom of it. She would be a mild-mannered and merciless interviewer, grinding very small.

'Not me, much as I'd love to. Gareth can't stand me, he'd probably resign. No, it needs someone who would carry authority with Gareth, whatever emerges from Timber Wolf, good or bad. It should be you. He might just accept your doing it. Might.'

The idea had already occurred to Charles, without his thinking seriously about it. As was often the case with half-formed ideas, it gained substance through having been suggested by someone else. It might also bring him a step closer to resolving a deeper, still unspoken worry he had about the case. Unspoken even now to Sonia. 'He wouldn't like it.'

'Would he have to know, until afterwards? You could contact Timber Wolf directly, pretending to be Gareth. Then you turn up instead.'

'But they communicate privately, don't they, as old friends? Not through Office comms to which we have access. And without a warrant we couldn't get across Gareth's private calls or texts or emails or WhatsApps or whatever they do. And to get a warrant on Gareth in this country we'd have to go through MI5 and the home secretary and I can't see we'd get it. There's not enough to make a national security case against him, even if we wanted to.'

'We do it from the other end. Timber Wolf. He's

a foreigner living abroad in whom we have a legitimate intelligence interest, if only in checking that he's playing straight with us. I can put in a request to Cheltenham and they can access Timber Wolf's comms – or his comms record – with a few clicks of a mouse.'

'But could they make a message from me appear to come from Gareth? And divert any reply to me?'

She shook her head. 'I know I'm a digital dinosaur but you're positively pre-Cambrian. That's bacon and eggs for Cheltenham. If they can fix your laptop so that it explodes when you switch on I'm sure they can redirect the odd text or two.'

'They can do that, can they? Blow it up?'

'So I've heard. Ask your opposite number.'

'Gareth will be pretty upset when he finds out I've seen Timber Wolf.'

'Don't wait for that. Tell him yourself, after the event. If it proves – as I suspect it will – that he's been a naughty boy, exaggerating intelligence, then he's no cause for complaint. If it proves him innocent then you simply say you had to do it so that you could reassure Whitehall with a clear conscience. And that will do no harm at all to his chiefly ambitions.'

'And meanwhile I say nothing about our doubts to Robin Woodstock but simply sound him out for retrospective clearance on the grounds that Timber Wolf is effectively a paid agent?'

'Got it in one, professor. Now, can we get out of here, please? I can feel my cholesterol going up just through looking at the place.'

In the Foreign Office Robin Woodstock was brisk. 'Sorry to rush. Morning meeting's been brought forward. The secretary of state's diary is a living exemplification of the second law of thermodynamics. The uncertainty principle, if I've got that right.' He grinned. 'Will ten minutes do or d'you want to rearrange?'

'We can do it in five.' That suited Charles. Less time meant less chance of the discussion widening to the point where he would either have to admit his doubts or mislead. He explained briefly.

Robin sighed and sat. 'So you think Timber Wolf is really a paid agent because of the amount he's given in unearned expenses and that if this came to light in Brussels it would make an already mighty stink even stinkier? No argument about that. Thus, if we want to continue the relationship we should seek clearance from the secretary of state and the prime minister so that they know the risks we're running and if the balloon goes up it's HMG that takes responsibility, not just us. By which I mean, you. What are those risks? How likely is it to come to light?'

'The EU itself has no intelligence service – yet – and

no serious counter-intelligence capability. It's unlikely that Timber Wolf or anyone else is under any sort of surveillance. But the French have active intelligence services and we know they take an interest in what goes on in Brussels. The Germans could but probably don't on principle – so far. It's unlikely that anyone would target Timber Wolf as a security threat but it's possible the French could stumble across it accidentally or that there could simply be gossip – the EU community in Brussels is very gossipy, as you well know, and they all know each other. Thus, the threat of exposure is small but the consequences would be serious, serious enough to threaten the government if Parliament had one of its fits of self-righteousness and got over-excited. It follows that the government should be told of the risks we're taking on its behalf and should formally say yes, go ahead, we accept them. Or no, risks unacceptable, stop it, close the case.'

Robin nodded. 'You're right, absolutely, you must submit on it. But I should tell you now that any such submission is very unlikely to be agreed. My comment will be that the case is not worth the political risk no matter how much we value the Timber Wolf stuff and I'm pretty certain that the ambassador in Brussels, the head of negotiations and the cabinet secretary – they'll all be consulted – will say the same.'

'And ministers?'

'Less predictable. The foreign secretary – not averse

to the odd bit of risk-taking as we know – might say
go ahead, the minister for Brexit could go either way,
the prime minister is cautious, as we also know, and
is unlikely to go against the collective view of the
mandarinate. But could be persuaded otherwise by
ministers. Which means you should submit a.s.a.p.,
expect it to be turned down and meanwhile suspend
meetings between Gareth Horley and Timber Wolf, as
you have already.' He stood and picked up a clipboard
and papers. 'Thanks, Charles, you were right to bring
it straight away, as soon as you became concerned. I
won't say anything to the secretary of state until we
get your submission.'

'Will do.' Charles was of course aware that he was
lying by omission. He didn't like misleading Robin but
was confident that the only way to resolve the issue
was to see Timber Wolf himself, which Robin was
most unlikely to go along with. Having the chief of
MI6 personally debrief an agent in Brussels who was
working against the EU would be a risk too far for
Whitehall. But Charles was rediscovering the exhila-
ration of calculated risk-taking, something he didn't
feel often enough these days.

He walked briskly back to Smith Square, detouring
as usual through Westminster Abbey's Palace Yard. It
was one of several places – the Chiltern beech-woods
where he had grown up, the sea view from his own
house on Scotland's west coast, a particular village

green in County Durham – that never failed to have a calming and reassuring mental effect, like the gentle rain of grace. He reached Head Office just in time to walk straight into the resources and finance meeting, which was in the boardroom. Jenny, his secretary, caught him as he went through.

'Sonia rang. She wants to speak urgently. Didn't say what it was about.'

'Ring her back and say I'll call as soon as I'm out of this meeting.'

Peter, his director of finance and resources, was as negative and nit-picking as usual. Charles, hating anything to do with money himself, easily forgave him that; it was what he was paid to be. Without that persistent brake bureaucracies had an inherent tendency to spread and add weight, spending ever more on maintaining themselves at the expense of what they were there to do. As a portion of the MI6 budget, support and administration costs rose faster than operational expenditure, mostly government-imposed. Health and safety, human rights and equalities legislation, diversity and deprivation monitoring and now something called inclusion assessments were costs imposed by Whitehall without any consideration of the effect on core business. Charles thought that the agencies and the MOD should be exempt from such legislation, and had said so more than once. He knew that each time he let his views be known there was heightened speculation about his retirement, and he knew too that his solitary struggle against the prevailing cultural and bureaucratic tide would get him nowhere. But he didn't mind, reasoning that he may as well say it while people were compelled to listen rather than afterwards, when he wouldn't be heard.

'We could monitor and assess ourselves into the ground until we do no spying at all,' he had complained at one board meeting, 'and no one would notice. But if ever we fail to account for how many women we have at senior grades or how many black and ethnic minorities we recruit, or the gender pay gap, all hell breaks loose.'

Peter's thin lips came as near to smiling as he permitted himself. 'More law means more sin, as St Paul observed. It must have been easier when you joined and the Service didn't officially exist, so didn't get caught up in all this stuff.'

'It was. And what about the Welsh? They must be an ethnic minority, surely? But we're never asked to monitor them.'

'You're not Welsh yourself by any chance?'

'No but Gareth is. Though he counts for two.'

They had laughed, including Gareth.

Not much chance of laughter this morning, Charles reflected as they took their places. He and Gareth had not spoken since the interview but there was no obvious change in Gareth's manner. He was as businesslike as usual and – also as usual – mildly but respectfully flirtatious with Pauline, the HR director. Charles observed this while thinking of Gareth's mistress in Brussels and of his wife Suzanne. He didn't suspect Gareth of designs on Pauline – too old and too plump – but could imagine him thinking that a little gentle flirtation might be a cost-free entry into her good opinion, so long as he didn't take it too far. Or maybe he just couldn't help himself, with any woman. When his and Gareth's eyes met Gareth nodded in friendly greeting, as usual. That too was politic, Charles thought, doing the same.

The meeting went as it usually did. Peter explained at length why everything was difficult, Pauline described problems with recruitment and retention, the director of IT and cyber spoke of the dire need for upgrades, Ian, the director of intelligence and analysis – Sonia's boss – spoke of the need to improve training and standards, Gareth stressed the importance of impressing on the Treasury examples of intelligence reports or covert actions that had saved public money. Charles announced that he was soon to meet the heads of MI5 and GCHQ to agree a co-ordinated approach to the Treasury. Each head of agency was to go along with a proposal for pooling resources that could be presented as efficiency savings; he asked each directorate to come up with one suggestion before the next meeting. He also asked

Peter to contrive frequent reasons to talk to the young Treasury official responsible for the single intelligence vote and to get her over to Smith Square so that she could meet staff and see the results of cuts.

Charles smiled at them all as he picked up his papers. 'Throughout my career I've complained about bureaucratic inefficiency and now I'm arguing against efficiency savings. Throughout my career I've argued that reductions in anticipated increases shouldn't be called cuts but now I'm doing just that, telling ministers that if they want to cut more they'll have to say which existing requirements they don't want us to meet. All of which should constitute further evidence – as if we needed it – that God has a sense of humour.'

'Dangerous game,' said Gareth. 'They might conclude they don't need any of it and then they wouldn't miss what they never see.' He looked at the director of intelligence and analysis. 'Which is why we've got to keep it all coming, don't you think, Ian?'

'And to think we joined SIS to spy,' said Charles. 'Another of God's jokes.'

'Sonia rang again,' said Jenny when he returned to his office. 'She wants to speak a.s.a.p.'

He closed his office door and rang while still on his feet. Sonia spoke with quiet urgency. 'Gareth's arranging another Timber Wolf meeting. Timber Wolf got in touch to say he needed to meet soon, that he'd got something special. His words. Gareth got back to him saying he was under pressure at the moment but would respond as soon as he could fix a date.'

'How do you know this?'

'They left messages on each other's mobiles.'

'But how do you know? We're not intercepting—'

Sonia sighed. 'You know I was to ask Cheltenham for a read-out of Timber Wolf's call history? Well, I asked for an update and these are the two latest calls. First thing this morning when you and I were in that awful cafe of yours, so well after you'd told him not to meet.'

'But how do you know what was said? A call history doesn't give you that. Unless you've got a warrant, which you haven't.'

'We don't need one to listen to Timber Wolf. He's a foreigner living abroad.'

'But you need a reason. He has to be logged as a target on security or intelligence grounds or whatever.' He worried that he might sound like some of the senior officers of his youth who had seemed to exist in order to stop things happening. 'I mean, I'm not trying to—'

'Economic well-being, protection and furtherance of. It's in the Intelligence Services Act. Timber Wolf has access to information of great economic impor-tance to this country. Therefore he's a legitimate intelligence target.'

'But who authorised it? You can't just do it off your own bat.'

'My director. Ian's authorising it retrospectively.'

'You mean he doesn't yet know about it.'

'I mean I have very long-standing contacts in GCHQ who trust me when I say authorisation is on its way. As it will be this afternoon, when I tell Ian you'd like it done.'

Charles could hear the smile in Sonia's voice. 'We haven't had this conversation. And of course we'll have to not have another one as soon as you hear that Gareth has fixed a date.'

'Which he may already have done. Gareth got back to him just before your meeting, this time by WhatsApp, which is encrypted, as perhaps even you know, Charles? And to get into that – if they can – is a whole new cryptographic ball game that I don't like to even ask them about. You know how Cheltenham keep that sort of thing very close to their chests. Don't want to use up my credit if it's not going to work. So, the chances are that Gareth's made a date but we don't know when.'

Charles replaced the receiver and stood for a while staring at the face of the Cumming clock. A plain face, clear Roman numerals, no twirls or embellishments, an open honest face, as honest as its maker.

The news surprised and disappointed him. For Gareth to cut operational corners was one thing, being lured into exaggeration by his own enthusiasm and ambition was another and calling agent payments expenses was a third: culpable faults all, but faults committed – as Churchill had put it – facing the enemy, trying to do the job, not running away from it. Faults worthy of censure, though ultimately forgivable. But to have arranged a meeting with Timber Wolf after Charles forbade it was deliberate deceit. It was personal, too. Charles felt let down. Gareth could have told him about the call; they would have considered what to do, Charles might have said go ahead but go carefully, then tried to cover his back by seeking Robin Woodstock's retrospective agreement. This was a betrayal, an unnecessary betrayal, as unnecessary as it was puzzling. Puzzling because Gareth wouldn't be able to report anything of the meeting without confessing he'd had it. So what could he hope to gain?

Chapter Seven

'The Tresco sub has been bounced back,' said Jenny. 'Our lawyers are happy with it but the Foreign Office lawyers want some changes. Our lawyers want to know if they have your support in resisting.'

'What kind of changes?'

'Something to do with ID verification. They're putting it in an email, which you haven't got yet because they're waiting to see whether MOD lawyers agree with them.'

'How many lawyers does it take to kill a terrorist?'

'About a dozen and rising.'

'Just as well I'm married to only one.' He asked her to check dates for directors' availability for a board awayday at the Castle, the south-coast training establishment.

'That's quite soon, isn't it? Not long since the last one.'

'This is an emergency one to take stock of resources

in case the Treasury cut up rough. We didn't go as far as worst-case scenarios this morning. With luck we won't need to, so don't put it in their diaries as a firm booking, just check for dates when they're available and when they're not. If it's difficult we can have a partial board, doesn't have to be a full one. In the next week, if possible.'

'If it's that soon you'll probably end up with a meeting of two.'

'The fewer the better so far as decisions are concerned.'

Michael Dunton rang from Thames House on the secure line. 'Your note on Sarah's godson has caused a flutter in the hen coops here. I've got the desk officer with me. No one's questioning your overall assessment of him as probably harmless but there's concern about the knives you say he's bought. It coincides with an odd conversation he's had with someone from this dodgy mosque group he's in with. Bit of an imposition, I know, but any chance you'd be able to pop over and listen to it? I would suggest Sarah too but our lawyers say we're not allowed to share such product outside the intelligence community, even for a Mrs C. Also, the team concerned want to take a closer look at her godson, technically closer, if you see what I mean, and it would help them a lot if you and Sarah could advise on arrangements.' Michael chuckled. 'Not sure whether I should apologise for distracting you with casework details or offer it as a chance to escape back to your operational past. Though you never had much luck with tech ops, if I remember rightly.'

'Always willing to revert to type and try again, so look at it as the latter. Anyway, it's not the only bit of casework around at the moment.'

'We owe you one, Charles. The desk will be in touch.'

Later, when he had the results of Jenny's diary research, Charles rang Sonia. 'Looks like Gareth's intending to go next Wednesday. It's the only day next week when he is completely unavailable. His diary is blanked out from Tuesday evening to Thursday morning with no explanation, which is unusual. Usually, whenever he has a Timber Wolf meeting he describes it as "Brussels Brexit briefing".'

'So if you're going to spring a surprise on Timber Wolf you'll have to see him before that, in time to stop Gareth going.'

'Or let him go, depending on what Timber Wolf reveals. Is Cheltenham ready with their box of tricks to turn me into Gareth, electronically speaking?'

'So long as it's by text or email, yes. Let me know what you want to say and they'll text it to Timber Wolf as if it's from Gareth and make sure the answer comes to us, not him. They have a name for it, this technique, but I can't remember it.'

'But what about any real texts Gareth is sending or receiving?'

'They'll go through. The clever stuff is done on Timber Wolf's phone. There may be some delay with his real messages while this exchange is on, but there often is anyway. He won't notice anything unusual.'

'He won't think it's odd that Gareth's texting after they've been using WhatsApp?'

'They use both. Their recent communications began with texts.'

'I'll need a briefing from you on the Brexit negotiations, everything you can find out about where they've got to and all that Timber Wolf has reported about them.'

'When will you go?'

'The sooner the better. It had better be a last-minute thing so far as Timber Wolf is concerned – Gareth must notionally be in Brussels unexpectedly and want to meet that day. If it's not last-minute Timber Wolf has more time to go back with alternative arrangements, perhaps by WhatsApp, and then we're scuppered.'

'What if he can't make it?'

'He has to, even if it's just a drink on his way home. Can you brief me tonight?'

That afternoon Shelley, Michael Dunton's desk officer, asked Jenny for an appointment to brief Charles. 'Tell her she can either hop across the river now or it will have to be some time next week.'

She arrived thirty minutes later, a fair, nervous-looking girl with a timid smile. Charles smilingly cut short her apologies for bothering him. 'Don't worry. The more favours I can do for Michael, the more I can ask in return. What exactly do you need from me?'

'We want to do a clandestine search of his house, a breaking and entry operation. We're doing the operational plan and Home Office warrant application at the moment. We'd do it of course when they're out but it would help enormously if you and Mrs Thoroughgood were able to guarantee when that would be and for how long. You don't know anything about their plans over the next two weeks, I suppose?'

'Not at all. Of course, you know she works full time for the Department for Education so she's fairly predictable, but he's self-employed and is probably here, there and everywhere, depending on where the work is. But why d'you need to break in? It's not just because of these knives?'

'It's partly that, yes, along with the fact that the other people in this mosque he's started going to get very excited every time there's a terrorist knife attack anywhere. They get all the details about it and analyse them and talk about how to do it better. Plus the fact that his wife is worried, as you reported.'

'So it's not just partly the knives, it is mainly the knives?'

'They're a large part of it, yes. But there's also this.'

She produced a small laptop from the briefcase she carried and inserted a memory stick. 'This is what the DG asked if you could come over and listen to. It's a phone conversation between Daniel and one of his mosque friends. We'd like to know whether you have any idea what it refers to. It could be knives but we're not sure.'

They listened three times to the short dialogue. A man who sounded of Indian-subcontinent origin rang Daniel and asked, without any preliminaries, if he had got 'it'. Daniel said yes, it looked good. The man asked if it was somewhere safe and Daniel said it was. The man said, 'See you on Friday,' and rang off.

'We're not sure what they're talking about,' said Shelley. 'Do you think it could be a knife?'

'Doesn't sound like it. It's a bit odd to say it looks good. A knife is a knife, pretty simple thing. And he's got more than one, of course.'

'Maybe he means it's fit for purpose, whatever that is.'

'Maybe. There's also the implication that he's hidden it. But we know his wife knows about the knives and anyway why would you hide a knife when you can just keep it in the kitchen drawer with others? Unless it's a special knife for hunting or skinning or something.'

'That's really why we want to get in there, to have a look and see whether there's anything else suspicious like guns or explosives or chemicals. Any signs of preparations for violence.'

Charles was still reluctant to imagine Daniel as a terrorist and unconvinced that he merited this level of investigation. But such assessments were MI5's business, not his. 'It's a pity we didn't know about this when we had them round for dinner. You could have done it then.'

Her nervous smile reappeared. 'Perhaps – we did wonder whether it would be possible for you to ask Daniel to come and look at doing some carpentering work on your house for you? Then we'd know where he'd be and for how long.'

'I suppose we could, yes.' He was wondering what Sarah would think of that. She had said something about rain coming under the back door when the wind was in that direction, which he had failed to notice.

'He's not got much work on at the moment, we know that. So he might be quite grateful. But perhaps you're not convinced he's that much of a threat?'

She had done her homework. Charles smiled. 'I guess I'm not, not as much as you. I was more reassured than alarmed when I chatted to him. He seemed more the evangelising convert than a would-be terrorist trying to conceal what he's up to. As for the knives – well, every kitchen has an array of lethal weaponry and as a carpenter he must already have sharp tools, Stanley knives and that sort of thing. Maybe he bought more knives because they needed them.'

'But it worried his wife.'

'Yes, that I can't explain away.' He shrugged. 'Well, you're the experts, you're seeing these things all the time. I'll have a word with Sarah and see if we can sort out some convincing household improvements. There's no great time pressure, is there?'

She looked relieved. 'Thank you, sir, that's very helpful. As for time pressure, although we've no indication of attack planning there are some indicators reflecting a pattern that in other cases have led to attack planning. We don't want to risk something happening and then have to admit that we had our suspicions all along but didn't do anything because it wasn't high-priority, as has happened before.'

Sarah was not happy about it when he rang her later. 'I understand their arguments but I find it very hard to believe that Daniel is planning to cut our throats, don't you? Or anybody's. He just doesn't seem that aggressive about it. And I feel really awkward about luring him out in order for his house to be burgled. I feel guilty enough about reporting on him anyway, as you know. God forbid that Deborah ever finds out.'

'Searched, not burgled. But there is some

joinery work we genuinely need doing, isn't there? That back door?'

'And those bookshelves you've been threatening to put up ever since we moved in.'

'Of course, yes.' He remembered them about once a month. 'I could get him round to have a look at both jobs.'

'Obviously, it would be nice to have them done. But I'd rather you did it. I suppose this sort of little deceit is all part of a day's work for you. Not that I'm criticising.'

He supposed it was. It hadn't occurred to him that anyone might see the setting-up of Daniel in this way as an ethical issue, albeit minor. Where deceit was a vocational requirement rather than a deformation as in business or finance or religions or other professions – even lawyers could be deceitful, he had found – it was easy to take it for granted as the common currency of daily life. If Daniel was not involved in terrorism, as Charles believed, he would never know his house had been searched, no harm would come of it and it would go a long way towards clearing the cloud of suspicion that hung over him. On the other hand, if he was found to be planning an atrocity it was better for him and for the world if he were prevented. Also, if he agreed to do the joinery work, he would earn some presumably much-needed money.

Daniel answered Charles's call immediately and they had a stilted but satisfactory conversation. Daniel was surprised and Charles awkward, conscious of injecting a note of false bonhomie. They agreed to meet at the house for half an hour the day after next.

Shelley was pleased and flustered when he told her. 'Thank you so much, CSS, that's most helpful. But it's very soon and I'm not sure we'll have time to get the warrant through.'

'Well, I'm afraid you'll just have to. I can't do it next week because I may be travelling and if we leave it until the week after there's more chance that what you fear might happen.'

'It's fixed,' said Sonia when she came up to Charles's office that evening. 'Timber Wolf's agreed to meet at the Rosticceria Fiorentino in the EU quarter, whatever that's called, at twelve-thirty on Monday. They've used it before. I've booked at table in Gareth's name.'

'But they'll realise it's not him when I turn up.'

'Get there early and they won't realise he's not joining you. You must have done this sort of thing before, surely?'

He had, with an East German in Athens during the Cold War. It hadn't worked; the East German walked out. 'Better shut the door in case Gareth's still in the building. Don't want him to walk in and see you here. He'll put two and two together and make – in this case – what they usually make.'

'He's gone home, as has his secretary. I checked.'

'Wine, whisky, G&T?'

'G&T, please, lemon, no ice.'

Charles pulled open the large lower desk drawer. 'No lemon, no ice.' While he poured the drinks she talked him through the latest round of negotiations with the EU. 'They seem to be making as much a meal of it as they can. The EU, I mean.'

'They always do. Then there's a compromise deal at the last minute. Usually. There may not be this time.'

'And Timber Wolf's reporting? Has it been consistently borne out?'

'Quite a lot of it has. If you list the main points in the negotiations alongside the main subjects of his reports there's a lot of carry-over. And he quotes plausible and revealing behind-the-scenes comments, which Whitehall readers love. They're usually the bits they remember best. But if you put all the Timber Wolf stuff alongside what's reported in the informed parts of the press and media, most of the time he's not really telling us anything new. He's elaborating on what we know or anticipate, all interesting so far as it goes but not exactly game-changing. There's nothing he predicts that goes contrary to the assumptions and expectations of the Brexit team. With one exception.' She sipped her drink. 'He quotes the EU negotiating team as being more complimentary in private about our lot, especially the prime minister, than we'd thought they were. Phrases like "unyielding but personally charming" and backhanded compliments such as "stubborn as a mule but rather cleverer" go down well with politicians because they like to read nice things about themselves, grudging respect from the enemy and all that. All of which adds to my suspicions that Gareth, knowing our susceptibilities, is reporting what he thinks we like to hear.'

'Gareth rather than Timber Wolf?'

'The phrasing is suspiciously familiar and colloquial. Stubborn as a mule, for example. I'm not sure in how many languages that phrase exists.'

'Me neither but Timber Wolf is Dutch and many Dutch speak excellent English. Better than we do, often as not.'

'True but there are plenty of other examples: phrases common in Whitehall – close of play, a.s.a.p., need to know, at the end of the day, including what you just said – often as not. There's even a reference to PQs, parliamentary questions. At the very least, I think Gareth is putting words into Timber Wolf's mouth. But I also suspect him of making some of it up. It's all too convenient.'

Charles booked to travel out on Eurostar on the Sunday, calling in a favour with the ambassador to attend a briefing in the embassy as his ostensible reason for being in Brussels. The ambassador was one of few cleared to read Timber Wolf product and knew it as a case run from London by Gareth, though he did not know Timber Wolf's identity.

'Own name or alias?' asked Jenny when making the booking.

'Own name. No point in anything else.' He had frequently operated under alias in the past but the Internet, social media and more sophisticated border checks had made it increasingly difficult to do so plausibly. There was still a security argument for chiefs of MI6 to use a travel alias and passport, in that a terrorist group that penetrated flight manifests might try to bring down a plane if they knew such a person was on it. But well-known ministers and officials daily used the Brussels Eurostar and Charles wanted his visit to appear as routine as possible.

'I'll put it down as own name official travel,' said Jenny, ignorant of his real reason.

'Also, I'm out of the office Friday lunchtime, meeting a carpenter at home, unless anything else crops up.'

'Unlikely. Lunch tempo seems to have dropped off a bit recently.'

'Perhaps we should revise it.' Despite the decline of the Whitehall lunch culture, official entertainment at senior levels continued because it was useful. But Charles, though an enthusiast for lunch, had done little of late. Many of the useful people were those he didn't really want to have lunch with and so he was leaving them to Gareth and other directors. He was getting lazy, he acknowledged. 'Draw up a list of those we owe and those we ought to cultivate but haven't,' he said. 'And include one or two for refreshment, like that Bank of England woman I first met years ago, the one who came last year.' He had found that people whose jobs were thought to be dull were often the most entertaining. 'And that actuary from HMRC. He was a real break in the clouds.'

Daniel's tape measure retracted viciously as he flicked the button. He stared at the patch of wall beneath the stairs, Charles looking over his shoulder. 'It's doable, yes, but you won't get the shelf space you thought, not if you want this under-stairs cupboard door to open fully. Depends how much you use it and what for.'

'Not much. Not often, anyway. Let's have a look.' There was a vacuum cleaner, brushes, a mop, a plastic bucket and a bowl. 'Maybe more than I thought. It's Mrs Wellbeloved's cupboard, our cleaner. How many shelves could you fit while allowing the door to open fully?'

'Two and a half. Three and a half if they're small books. There's nowhere else we can put them?'

As they explored the house Charles thought of the search team in Daniel's at that moment. They'd have picked his locks, disabled his alarm – with ease, apparently – and filmed everything to ensure they left it exactly as it was. When Daniel left Westminster he would be followed by a surveillance team, who would warn the search team if he was heading for home. There was a back-up plan to block his street with a broken vehicle, or stage an accident, in case he or Akela were lost by surveillance and turned up unexpectedly. MI5 were nothing if not thorough.

'Could do floor-to-ceiling shelves here,' said Daniel as they stood on the landing upstairs. 'So long as you find somewhere else for that trunk.'

It was an old seaman's trunk that had been in Sarah's family for generations. 'I'd have to take advice on that.'

'Or just four shelves above it if it stays where it is.'

Daniel had been there only about half an hour; the search team really wanted a clear hour. Charles had already shown Daniel the leaking back door. 'Tea or coffee?' he offered. 'There's soup and bread too if we fancy it.'

'I'm good, thanks.'

'But you need to eat. I'm going to have some. It's vegetable soup.'

'Okay, may as well. Got out of the habit of eating in the middle of the day but no harm, I guess.'

They ate at the kitchen table. Daniel drank water, Charles reluctantly following suit. They talked about self-employment, finding business, bad debts and the attractions of carpentry. Daniel had initially been attracted by the feel and smell of wood, the skills had not been difficult to acquire, given patience and application, and modern tools made the work much easier.

'I admire the older carpenters,' he said, 'the blokes who did it all with hand tools, no power or anything. The skill, the artistry sometimes, the attention to detail. It's wonderful to behold when you come across old work hidden behind walls or in lofts. In fact, I've started collecting old tools from boot sales or wherever. Sometimes people I'm working for give me odd bits and pieces, old planes and drills and so on. They're attractive objects in themselves. I polish them up but occasionally I use them if I'm not in a hurry or I'm doing a bit of work for myself. Keeps my hand in. You know that old saying, it's a bad workman that blames his tools? Well, the truth, the real truth of that, lies in the fact that in the olden days craftsmen made their own tools.'

He continued with an enthusiasm hitherto reserved for his religion. It was easier to share, lacked aggression and made him more likeable. Charles was congratulating himself on having got through lunch without a sermon when Daniel broke off and said, 'But the important thing is, it is all to the glory of Allah, my work. That is really why I do it. The Prophet – peace and blessings be upon Him – has given me this gift that I may work to the will of Allah to bring about a better world.'

Charles nodded, wondering whether medieval craftsmen building the monasteries might have spoken like that. More likely, perhaps, to talk about themselves in this way were seventeenth-century Puritans, scorched by enthusiasm. Beneath it all, he was beginning to feel, was a Daniel he could like, but enthusiasm – religious or political – was always a barrier to full intercourse. Acquiescing, allowing oneself to appear to share it – if only by not opposing – felt like an imposition, a demand by the enthusiast that the world conform to his or her beliefs.

He got up and cleared away the soup bowls. The search team should be finished by now. 'Going back to your business, it must take time to build up a customer base but it sounds as if you've made a good start.'

'I have a difficult decision coming up and I'm praying for guidance. I have to decide whether to carry on building up my business or whether I should travel now while the business is fairly small and return to start again later.'

'Travel?'

'To help other Muslims, to bring aid to the suffering.'

'Join an aid convoy, you mean?'

'Something like that. Not necessarily a convoy.'

'What about Akela? You were talking of starting a family . . .'

'That, too, that's another complication. The resolution is in the hands of Allah. I'm praying to learn what His will is.'

He sounded like someone waiting to hear whether normal service had been resumed on the railway. Charles wanted to ask when he expected to hear but was wary of sounding frivolous. 'Have you made any plans yet?'

'I'm waiting for a sign.'

'We'd better get these shelves agreed before you go, if we can.' Daniel summarised his proposals and gave an estimate, which Charles agreed subject to confirming with Sarah that it was what she wanted. As Daniel left he paused on the doorstep.

'Thank you for this. It's kind of you to think of me. It may be a while before I can do it.'

'It's not just kindness. We need it done and we'd much rather have you around to do it than some stranger.'

'Any good deed is a blessing. May the peace of Allah be upon you.'

They locked eyes again for a moment. Daniel's were full and serious. Charles inclined his head. 'Thank you, Daniel.'

He next rang Shelley. 'He's just left. I think he's going straight home by tube.'

'That's fine. The team is out now and we've pulled back surveillance.'

'Did they find anything?'

'I'll hear when they get back and let you know.'

'He's hoping to travel, maybe soon. Aid to suffering Muslims. We didn't go into where. I assume the Middle East rather than Chechnya or China. Seems pretty serious about it. I'll report in writing when I'm back in the office.'

'Thank you, CSS, this could be very important.'

Chapter Eight

'Sorry, Marigold, but I'm not sure I followed everything you said. My fault entirely. Could you bear to go through it again?'

Marigold was a short energetic woman in her forties with black hair and vivid red lipstick. She was the Health and Safety Advisor. H&S was embedded deep in the administrative structure, a part of his responsibility that Charles was happy to know little about provided it enabled core tasks without impinging too much upon them. He picked up occasional groans about it but no one complained directly. He had asked Gareth at a board meeting whether it was a problem.

'More containable irritant than operational inhibitor,' Gareth had said. 'As yet, people moan about it and the wretched procedures delay things but it hasn't actually stopped anything. Personally, I ignore it and advise others to do the same if they complain. What H&S don't know they can't bugger up.'

'Leaves us legally vulnerable,' said the legal advisor.

Gareth smiled. 'Calculated risks. So long as we can show they're reasonable.'

Charles was happy to avert his gaze, another example of complacency, he now acknowledged to himself as Marigold began to expound. She enjoyed expounding. 'The essence, CSS, is that whenever anyone leaves Head Office, an overseas station or any other Service premises on operational business there has to be an H&S assessment of potential risk and measures taken to mitigate it. That's why we have Form HS37/4/A. Most officers complete them online but there is a procedure for people who like yourself find' – she struggled momentarily – 'who like yourself prefer to do them by hand. When an operational trip is logged it comes up automatically on our screen in H&S and we check that there is a completed HS37/4/A and chase it up if there isn't. Now, I know your secretary logged this as an official not an operational trip but our system automatically logs any trip by CSS as operational on the grounds that CSS is an obvious target for terrorists and other ill-wishers and so all his or her official trips should be treated as if they were operational. And so I'm afraid I have to ask you to complete an HS37/4/A.' She held up the form and laughed nervously.

Charles looked at her. She was not obviously

ill-willed and probably had no greater sense of her own importance than was normal among people whose job was to stop other people doing things. 'So, H&S gets notification of anyone going on an operational trip – who, where and when?' He tried to sound curious rather than critical.

She nodded happily. 'Yes, it seems to work quite well on the whole. We don't know who they're seeing, of course. Only the code names.'

'Only the code names.'

'Yes. And then when we've signed it off it's counter-signed by the legal advisor or his or her representative.'

'I suppose the system was designed for stations such as Kabul and Baghdad where there's a real ter-rorist risk?'

'Exactly, yes.'

'But I'm going to Brussels.'

'Yes, well, obviously there aren't the same risks as in those places but there are some and so it's important to conduct an H&S assessment in the light of what's happened in the past and of what might happen in the future.'

'Such as a bomb on Eurostar?'

'Yes, indeed, yes.'

He leaned across and took the form from her. 'And how would this save me if there were?'

'Well, it would show that we were at least aware of the risk and had taken it into account. It's all part of our duty of care. You might, in the light of the risk assessment, have decided to fly or go by ferry.'

'Does there need to be a risk assessment for the embassy I'm visiting?'

'Which embassy?'

'Ours, the British.'

'Oh.' Marigold's red lips formed an almost perfect circle. 'Oh, I am sorry, CSS, I do apologise. If you're going to a British embassy that is classed as British official premises just like going to a ministry in Whitehall here you don't need to complete HS37/4/A at all. The notification we got just said "embassy visit" and I assumed it was a foreign one.'

'So, if I were going to the Luxembourgian embassy I would need to complete it in case that was a dangerous place, but as it's ours I don't?'

'Exactly, yes. Or, of course, if you were doing anything else there like meeting someone, anything operational.'

Charles handed back the form. 'Thank you, Marigold. I should have been more aware of all this. You've opened my eyes.'

His next meeting that Friday afternoon was with Pauline, director of HR, which he still had to stop himself calling Personnel. Pauline, like Marigold, was not a career SIS officer but had been recruited from the Department for Work and Pensions. She was competent and conscientious. After they had gone through the usual gamut of recruiting and retention figures, the possibility of another Treasury-funded early retirement scheme, senior management gender balance, the Service's age profile and sickness records, she coughed and said, 'There is another issue, CSS, which we've been watching for a while but which I haven't mentioned before because it hadn't come to a head. It still hasn't, not really, but neither has it gone away. So I thought I ought to raise it.'

Charles waited. She coughed again and shifted in her seat. 'It's a sexual harassment matter, I'm afraid. It is alleged that one of our board colleagues has been harassing one of his junior staff.'

'Not Gareth Horley, by any chance?'

She looked surprised. 'Yes, were you aware ... ?'

'There have been rumours in the past, that's all. What does the girl – presumably it is a girl? – allege?'

'The *female*' – Pauline stressed the word, correctively – 'is not herself the source of the allegations. It's a friend in whom she has confided. The friend is making them on her behalf, although without her knowledge.'

'What is Gareth alleged to have done?'

'Nothing physical, no touching-up or anything like that. No propositions either, not directly. It's his manner, apparently, the way he says things. He makes the victim uncomfortable. They call him the bus conductor, his female staff, that is.'

'Why? Are bus conductors notorious for ... ?'

'No, it's because he's always jiggling the loose

change in his pocket when he's talking to them. The older ones coined the phrase – so to speak – because they can remember buses with conductors and change. But that's got nothing to do with the allegation, of course. It's difficult to know what to do about it because the victim hasn't actually—'

'The complainant hasn't complained?'

'Not yet, no.'

'Can the girl— person who has complained on her behalf get her to come forward?'

'We've tried that but the trouble is the victim doesn't know her friend has reported to us and her friend doesn't want her to know. We can't act without a complaint, you see. We could ask the victim if she's suffered any form of harassment but her friend doesn't want us to do that because she thinks that will point the finger at her.'

'And the allegation – the allegation that isn't, yet – is about innuendo and suggestive remarks, is it?'

'I think it's more a question of tone.'

'Tone.' Charles looked up at the clock again, though not to check the time. 'Have you ever noticed anything in his tone?'

'Not with me, no. He's always been very – well, nice. Straightforward, friendly.'

Charles recalled the mildly flirtatious attentiveness Gareth usually deployed with Pauline. 'What would you like me to do?'

'Well, it's awkward, of course. We can't speak to Gareth ourselves without possibly blowing our source, as it were, but you know him quite well and I wondered if you could perhaps have a word with him about it, informally?'

'About his tone with all women or this one in particular, the un-named one?'

'That's difficult because we can't do anything to single her out. Perhaps you could just say there's been a complaint and you don't want to name names?'

'But there hasn't been a complaint.'

'Not directly, no.'

'And it's just his tone?'

'Tone can be important.'

'But we can't say with whom.' Charles could imagine how the conversation would go. With luck, existing concerns about Gareth would swamp this before action was required. 'I'm away on a visit in the early part of next week. I'll speak to him when I get back.'

The Rosticceria Fiorentino was not far from the Berlaymont, the headquarters of the EU Commission where Timber Wolf worked. It had cheerful plastic tablecloths and plaques on the walls commemorating the founding fathers of the EU who had patronised it when planning their project. Plaques apart, the interior appeared not to have changed greatly since those days; the menu looked like good basic Italian pasta and meat. Table separation was not ideal but just about adequate. It was unlikely that Timber Wolf would run into colleagues, who were said to favour the Barbanera with its fish and private garden, but it would not have seemed an odd place for him to use if he had. A good choice, no less than Charles would have expected from Gareth. When booking the table in Gareth's name, Sonia said she had been asked whether he wanted his usual one, the corner one. He knew from Gareth's notes that Timber Wolf was always punctual, so he deliberately arrived five minutes late. If he had been first Timber Wolf might have thought Gareth wasn't there or he might have hesitated to join Charles, compelling Charles to explain while they were both on their feet, attracting attention.

It was a grey drizzly day and while being relieved of his coat and umbrella he had time to identify Timber Wolf. It was not difficult; from Gareth's notes and from open sources researched by Sonia he knew to look for a big, heavily-built man, getting on for six and a half feet tall with long sloping shoulders, wide hips, massive haunches, spade-like hands bristling with red hair and a belly betokening many Brussels lunches. He saw now that his head was enormous, his auburn hair greying and thinning. His face was round and flat, good-natured, creased with laughter-lines. Ears, lips, nose and eyebrows were all prominent but his grey-green eyes seemed disproportionately small despite magnification by heavy, black-framed glasses. Charles approached without waiting for the waiter. 'Mr Rutte?'

The bushy eyebrows arched above the glasses. 'Eddie Rutte, yes.'

'I'm Charles Thoroughgood. I work with Gareth. At the last minute today he was unable to make it and asked me to come in his place, since you had indicated you had something special to discuss.' He held out his hand. Timber Wolf half rose from his chair as they shook, enveloping Charles's hand firmly and warmly. Charles pulled back the empty chair and went to sit, inadvertently initiating a brief comedy as they each bobbed the same way to avoid the other. They both smiled.

'Gareth is okay, I hope? Nothing has happened to him?'

'No, no, he's fine. He sends best wishes and regrets. He has to cope with an operational emergency in the Far East – you know he oversees operations worldwide? – which calls for urgent decisions and delicate negotiations with ministers. He'll be in touch to arrange another meeting soon but meanwhile was anxious not to put you off since your business sounded urgent, too. He asked me to pass on love to Anne-Marie from him and Suzanne and their best wishes for a speedy recovery.' Sonia had discovered that Timber Wolf's wife had recently had a knee operation.

'That's kind of him. Please say that she is walking

normally and already looking forward to skiing in the New Year. Perhaps this time Gareth and Suzanne will be able to join us?'

They were interrupted by the arrival of menus and water. Charles sensed the rapid working of Timber Wolf's mind behind the benign features and clever little green eyes. He had done well to conceal what must have been a shock and would now be asking himself whether the reason given for Gareth's non-appearance was genuine, whether Charles could be trusted, whether he should tell him what he had wanted to tell Gareth so urgently, perhaps even whether Charles would pay him as Gareth had.

'Gareth and I usually share a lunchtime bottle,' said Timber Wolf. 'Will you ... ?'

'I was hoping you'd say that. It's a relief to find that Brussels maintains proper lunching traditions. If it died out here there'd be no hope for the rest of the world. You know the wines. You choose.'

They were both having steak. Timber Wolf chose a Chianti Classico. 'Mr Thoroughgood—'

'Charles, please.'

'And I am Ed. Big Ed, they call me.' He laughed. 'Tell me, Charles, you are – you must be, Gareth often mentions you – his boss?'

Charles nodded.

'So I am lunching with the big cheese, the chief of MI6? This is a great honour, something I never expected.'

'I'm very happy the opportunity arose. I've heard a lot about you from Gareth. He's fond of you.' He paused as a man and a woman squeezed past on their way to another table. 'And he greatly values your advice. He thinks highly of it. As do I.'

'He shows them to you, the reports he writes?'

'Indeed he does. Not only me but people higher up the food chain.'

'How high?' Timber Wolf's expression was still genial but his question came just a little too quickly and sharply.

'As high as it goes, right up to the top.' It was almost possible to watch that little nugget go down as it was tasted, swallowed and digested. Of course, normal vanity would guarantee appreciation – everyone liked their offerings to be appreciated – but Timber Wolf's evident relish suggested something beyond that, such as the need for precision in reporting. There was another pause while he tasted the Chianti. 'Now tell me,' Charles continued with lowered voice, 'what is it you wanted to tell Gareth so urgently? I'm pretty well up with what you reported at your last meeting but the negotiations have moved on since then. It's about them, I assume?'

'It's about the money, what is acceptable. As you know, there's the British offer down there' – he lowered his hand, palm down, towards the floor – 'and the EU demand up here.' He raised his hand high above the table, grinning. 'Everyone assumes but no one says there must be a compromise about here.' He laid his palm flat on the table. 'Especially the British side because you are always pragmatists, but because you are choosing to leave the Commission thinks it is not for the EU to compromise further. But it is coming under pressure from European governments to reach a compromise.'

'Which governments?'

'Mostly the smaller countries. My own, for example, and Denmark – which has already gone public, as we've seen. And the Eastern Europeans.'

'Aren't they supposed to be hard-line on this because they want more EU money and don't want the EU to be poorer?'

'That is the public stance but privately, beneath the table, as it were' – he grinned again and pointed beneath the table – 'they are saying some money is better than no money. They worry that Britain is serious about walking away if there is no deal.'

'But France and Germany, who will run the EU by themselves once Britain is gone, say no compromise, don't they?'

'Again, that is the public perception.'

All public thus far, Charles was thinking. All this could be found in the media, including the claim that the Eastern Europeans spoke differently in private. Although, to be fair to Timber Wolf, that had so far surfaced only as speculation. 'But which Eastern

European countries? All of them in common cause or only one or two?'

Timber Wolf shook his big head. 'I don't know, not yet. But I hope to find out. So far it is mentioned only in general terms.'

'Mentioned by whom?'

'By one of Michel Barnier's team.'

'That's very interesting, thank you.' Charles tried to sound appreciative before continuing, gently, 'Which one?'

He couldn't be sure whether he perceived or imagined awkwardness on Timber Wolf's part. He might have been unprepared for Charles's persistence, or perhaps felt he was crossing a line by naming names. Names of officials did not feature much in Gareth's write-ups. Timber Wolf's hesitation, if it was one, was only momentary before he named one of Barnier's team, a French official. Charles thought he had seen the name in the press. He nodded. 'Thank you. Were you with him when he said this or did someone tell you he'd said it?'

'I was there, I was with him.'

'Where?' There was a natural pause now as their steak arrived. Timber Wolf shrugged and held up his knife and fork as if it were an impossible question. 'Gareth is bound to ask me,' Charles added with an ameliorating smile.

'In Barnier's outer office. I was there to discuss a

brief I had written. He didn't say it to me, he was talking to other members of his team. I just overheard it, that's all.'

'When was this?'

'Let me think – Monday – no, Tuesday. Definitely Tuesday.'

Charles wanted to go on, to nail the occasion down – the exact words used, names of others present, their reactions to it, what else was said, whether it was regarded as received opinion or as something new. And what was the brief that Timber Wolf had written, for whom and what did it say, had he a copy? But he didn't want to provoke exasperation. Timber Wolf was clearly unused to being pressed on his sources, which was disappointing. Charles had thought better of Gareth's debriefing skills. He changed tack. 'Going back to France and Germany and their no-compromise approach. You said that was the public perception. Were you suggesting that it's wrong?'

'That is why I wanted to see Gareth. This is what I wanted to tell him.' He poured them both more wine and leaned forward, his elbows on the table. 'I have heard from someone who is in a position to know that the French and German presidents have privately agreed a compromise figure that they would accept. But it is to remain strictly private because they are still trying to get Britain to come up to here.' He raised his hand palm downwards again, smiling.

'What is the figure?'

'I don't know, he didn't say, but I think it is about here.' He lowered his hand until it was about halfway down to the table. 'It is above the British maximum and below the EU minimum. If the British can come up to it, the EU will settle. Then both parties can have a good deal.'

'Who told you this?'

'I am sorry, Charles, I cannot tell you. It is more than my life is worth. I could not even tell Gareth in confidence. But one day I shall, I promise.'

Charles decided it was time for some handwork theatricals of his own. He put down his glass and sat back, shrugging, pursing his lips and raising his hands in a gesture of hopeless appeal. 'I'm sorry, Eddie, this is not good enough. I won't even report it. Un-sourced information is no good to us. We have to be able to validate it. If the British government is to increase its offer by many billions then it needs to know not only that it will be accepted but what it will get in return. And in order to feel sure of that it needs to know where the information comes from.'

'But it will get everything in return, it will get the trade deal it wants.'

Charles lowered his hands and leaned forward so that they were elbow to elbow. 'Who said it and how much?'

Timber Wolf exhaled, his warm breath wafting

across to Charles. 'You are being very hard with me. You put me in a difficult position.'

As Gareth clearly never did, Charles thought. 'But you do understand, Eddie, why un-sourced information is no use to us?'

Timber Wolf looked down at his plate, shaking his head. When he looked up again he was smiling broadly enough for his small eyes to disappear behind folds of flesh. 'I will not say a name but I can tell you enough for you to work it out. I think you will find it is a credible and authoritative source.' He paused, looking for a reaction. Charles did not react. He went on. 'The presidents of France and Germany each have a chef de cabinet. You know that, of course. Well, it was one of them.' He sat back.

'When?'

'Tuesday – no, Wednesday – before I contacted Gareth, anyway. You will have seen that the two presidents met in Paris. It was in all the papers. You can check it. Their chefs de cabinet accompanied them.'

'Were you there?'

There was another hesitation. 'Yes.'

'Where?'

'In the Élysée.'

'What exactly did he say, the one who spoke?'

'He said, "If the British will meet Barnier halfway we would, of course, tell him to do the deal."'

'Who did he say it to?'

'The other one, the other chef de cabinet.'

'And what did he say?'

'He nodded.'

'Is that all? He didn't say anything else?'

'They went into their meeting. I wasn't included.'

'What were you doing there?'

'I was accompanying my boss. He attended the meeting. It was a private briefing for the two presidents on future EU strategy for dealing with the Eastern European countries. There has been no publicity about it.'

'Who else was at the meeting?

'I don't know. I don't know them all.' There was a hint of exasperation in his tone.

'Which of the chefs de cabinet said it?' Both were well-known official figures and it wasn't essential to know this, but Charles persisted because he wanted to condition Timber Wolf to never holding back on sourcing.

Timber Wolf again shook his head and smiled. 'It is very difficult for me, this.'

'I understand that, Eddie. But it's also very important. I need to know.' Charles raised his left hand. 'You don't need to mention a name. Just indicate whether it was the French – this hand – or the German.' He held up his right hand alongside it.

Timber Wolf nodded at Charles's right, saying nothing.

'Thank you, Eddie. Thank you very much.' It was time for another change of tack. 'By the way – talking of Anne-Marie – I think Gareth wants to arrange an early Christmas lunch for all four of you before the Christmas rush starts, so long as Anne-Marie's knee is up to it.' This was a lie, intended to suggest normality and a future.

'It will be. Ballerinas suffer many injuries in later life but they are also very resilient. Tell him we must fix it soon. Christmas lunch begins early in Brussels.'

'I'm sure he'll be in touch about it.' He wasn't, of course; it would depend on whether the case continued and, if it did, whether it included Gareth. And that would depend on what else emerged. So far it was inconclusive. There was no sign of the fabrications Sonia suspected; Timber Wolf really did seem to have the sub-sources Gareth said he had, even if he wasn't accustomed to naming them. But Charles felt he couldn't yet rule out exaggeration. He knew exactly how Gareth would write it up and imagined it for himself, making the whole thing more meaningful and clear-cut, thus more convincing, than it actually was:

On 14 October M. Macron, the French president, and Angela Merkel, the German chancellor, met in Paris for one of their regular bilaterals. Also present were senior EU officials, including some associated with the Brexit negotiations. Speaking in confidence to a British official he knew to be an SIS officer, one of those present reported a conversation between the French and German chefs de cabinet in which the latter proposed that if the British were to increase their offer on the so-called divorce payment to halfway between the current level and what the EU is demanding, then the German and French governments should ensure that the EU accepted it. The French chef de cabinet agreed that that should be their joint position.

Source was confident that this would become the agreed position between the two governments but did not know whether the EU negotiators had yet been instructed to compromise.

That would read well enough, horse's-mouth stuff with direct access and bang up to date. It would play to the government's default position, which seemed to be to compromise and then compromise again, and it implied the actual cost of a deal, something hitherto only guessed at. Whether to offer that amount or not would be a political decision but ministers would at least feel they knew the EU's real thinking. It would give them time to prepare Parliament and the public for a settlement costing the country far more than they had originally suggested but also significantly less than the EU's public demand. It would be the kind of compromise familiar to anyone who had bought a house or car and it could be made to sound reasonable. It would also save the taxpayer billions.

But it couldn't be trusted, not fully. There was less to it than met the eye. When he had asked Timber Wolf why he was there the response – that he was part of the team sent along to provide technical briefing if required – was too vague and too off-pat to be convincing. It was also at variance with what he had previously told Gareth – that he had nothing to do with the negotiating team but was responsible for long-term strategic thinking. And there was no context to the German chef de cabinet's alleged remark – did it come out of the blue or was it part of a discussion of the negotiations? If so, what had preceded it? Its status was also unclear. Did it reflect German government thinking, or existing joint thinking with the French, or was it speculative political musing that hadn't been translated into policy and might never be? Or was it merely the personal opinion of the speaker and did the French official, in nodding, indicate agreement, or was he merely acknowledging that he'd heard it? And if it was a serious proposition, was anyone actually doing anything about it?

Charles waited until they had their coffees before mentioning money. 'Your expenses. I know Gareth is punctilious about settling them and I daren't go back without having done so. How much do we owe you?'

'My expenses? I have none, of course, apart from shoe leather. But if you mean my pay, I thank you. The same as usual.' He wiped his lips with his napkin.

'Remind me, please.'

Timber Wolf was clearly unembarrassed by discussing money. He named a sum that was half what the file said he was paid each meeting. When Charles repeated it, questioningly, he said, 'Yes, of course, that is the salary Gareth suggested and which I agreed. I think it is not too much?'

'Not at all, it's fine. I was just checking I'd got it right. Cash, isn't it?'

'Gareth insisted. I would have preferred payments into my account but he said they would be traceable if there were an inquiry. I agreed with that, too.'

Charles had twice that sum in euros in a sealed envelope in his jacket pocket. It would be awkward to open it and halve it in front of Timber Wolf. He could do it in the loo but it would be obvious that the envelope had been opened. Instead he took out the envelope and put it on the table as if getting it out of the way while he fished for his wallet. 'There's twice the usual in there. It's a bonus.'

The envelope disappeared beneath Timber Wolf's large hand. He smiled. 'Thank you, Charles. I knew this information would be important for you.'

'It is greatly appreciated. Greatly.' He let Timber Wolf leave first while he settled the bill, standard practice in order not to be seen together on the street.

The rain had stopped and Charles walked back to the British embassy through busy wet streets. He needed to walk in order to absorb his disappointment.

Despite Gareth's infidelities – the current mistress was by no means the first – and his exaggeration of intelligence, he had thought him honest where the Service was concerned, that a line could be drawn between the personal and the professional. Exaggeration was one thing, emblematic of self-promotion and a desire for results; calling Timber Wolf's salary expenses was reprimandable but understandable in terms of his fear that the case might otherwise be closed down; but fiddling the payments, keeping half for himself, was more serious than personal or petty dishonesty, more serious than culpable stupidity, more serious than the criminality involved. It suggested something congenital. Gareth had no need for the money. He was paid well and should have known that his deceit would come to light one way or another. It was not lack of intellectual capacity or moral awareness, or failure of rational process, or even an excess of greed. It must be an aspect of character, and was therefore indivisible. That meant that the demarcation between the personal and the professional, which Charles had long assumed, was an illusion. He had known two traitors in his career and had been forced to recognise that there was no such demarcation in their lives, but he had still – complacently, it now appeared – assumed it existed in everyone else's, including his own. Even now he didn't believe that Gareth was another traitor; but he had the potential become one.

He didn't trouble the ambassador again when he reached the embassy but went straight up to the SIS station. Following the ambassador's briefing that morning they had organised a presentation for him in the station, showing they were doing the right things; he had said the right things. Now they were back to normal routines. He commandeered a desk and screen and sent a top-secret, addressee-only email to Sonia, summarising the main points of the lunch and asking her to meet him on return. Then he emailed Jenny, asking her to set up separate meetings the following morning with Robin Woodstock in the Foreign Office and with his own head of security. Jenny reported that the Op Tresco submission was now back with the Foreign Office lawyers.

He was about to leave for the Eurostar, bag in hand, when Sarah rang his mobile. 'Daniel's gone missing. I've just heard from Anya, who had it from Akela.'

'When, how long since?'

'Yesterday morning. He was there when she left to visit her family and when she came back he was gone. He had taken a travelling bag and some clothes. She hasn't heard from him since.'

'What about the knife or knives he bought?'

'I didn't ask. Anya didn't mention them.'

Afterwards, Charles put down his bag. 'I'm afraid I need to use your system again,' he told the head of the station. 'This time to get on to MI5.'

Chapter Nine

It was after hours by the time Charles reached London. He went straight to his office, asked Sonia to come up and see him, then rang Michael Dunton, who was also still at work.

'All we know is what you said the sister-in-law said to Sarah,' Michael said. 'Shelley has checked his phone and computer and social media and all that and there's nothing, nothing at all. Which is unusual. D'you think he's taken fright after your session with him?'

'I don't see why he should've. It wasn't exactly threatening. Quite the opposite.'

'Let's hope it's not the quiet before the storm, that he's not holed up somewhere planning an attack.'

'What about his friends, the little group he's in with?'

'All normal, apparently. No one missing, nothing untoward, no one's mentioned him. Perhaps he's walked under a bus or jumped in the river.'

'That would be a sin too far, unless he did it while defending the Faith. We – Sarah or I – could go back to his sister-in-law, see if we can get any more.'

'Much appreciated. I'll ask Shelley to get in touch.'

Charles put down the phone and looked up to see Gareth standing in the doorway, listening. The private office was unmanned, so there was no access control. Gareth grinned. 'Trouble at t'mill?'

'All is not quiet on the home front.'

While Charles explained Gareth walked in and sat. He looked calm and relaxed. When Charles finished he said quietly, 'You've been to see Timber Wolf.'

It was predictable that Gareth would hear from Timber Wolf about the meeting but Charles hadn't anticipated it would be so soon. He should have told Gareth himself immediately, he now realised, rather than leaving it until the following day, when he had intended to confront him with his dishonesty. It was partly because he hadn't decided precisely what he would say and do about that, wanting to discuss it with his head of security first, that he hadn't anticipated that Gareth and Timber Wolf would be in touch so quickly, there being no obvious need. Lacking a planned response, he fell back on a mixture of truth and lie. 'I went to see Robin Woodstock to tell him about the payments and sound him out unofficially on the chances of clearance. He reckoned there wasn't a cat in hell's chance we'd get clearance to run a paid agent in the EU Commission at the present time. Whether we see Timber Wolf as an agent or not, his accepting money implies he sees himself as one and Robin had no doubt that the rest of the world would too if it came to light. He wanted the case closed immediately and forbade further contact. I persuaded him to let me see Timber Wolf for one meeting in order to assess his veracity and to gauge how he sees what he's doing. I have to report back tomorrow morning.'

'And your verdict?'

Sonia appeared briefly in the open doorway, saw who was there and disappeared. Gareth had his back to her.

'It's clear to me he sees himself as a paid agent,' said Charles. 'What that says about his motivation, I'm not sure, but it must be part of it. It was clear too that he sees himself not only as your agent – though you clearly have a strong personal relationship and he's obviously fond of you – but as our agent, an agent of SIS. He had no qualms about taking money from me, nor who I was nor what I represent. He sees himself as in a relationship with us, SIS as an institution, as well as with one – now two – individuals in it.' He paused. Gareth did not react at the mention of money but continued to gaze steadily, his hands resting on the arms of the chair, his legs crossed. The only very slight movement was a vibration in the polished toecap of the shoe on his crossed leg. His Trickers shoes,

Charles couldn't help recalling. 'As for what he reports, it appears to me to be genuine – so far as it goes. He seems to have genuine access. But he was reluctant to name his sources. I had to push him.'

'So I haven't made it all up? You conclude I'm not a fabricator after all?'

'Perhaps an unconscious embroiderer on occasion, overwriting, putting words into his mouth.'

'What in other circumstances might be called prompting a clearer and more explicit expression of meaning.'

'I'm seeing Robin Woodstock first thing tomorrow. I shall try to persuade him that we should go for clearance, that this is one for ministers to decide.'

'No chance he'd agree to us carrying on as we are with payments delayed until after the negotiations are over?'

'No.'

Gareth raised his hands, palms upwards. 'Then it's over, case over. He's right on clearance – we'll never get it. Nothing we can say will make it any less of a political risk and this government's nothing if not risk-averse.'

'You're almost certainly right but it's worth a try. Nothing ventured nothing gained. There's no chance of further meetings without it – mine was strictly a one-off – so there's nothing to lose by trying.' He did not say that there was an unmentioned alternative;

that if his private suspicion could be verified ministers might see it as a risk worth taking. Even, perhaps, an opportunity to be seized. 'Whisky?'

Gareth shook his head and stood abruptly. 'Let me know what happens.'

Charles waited until he heard the sound of the lift before ringing Sonia. 'Coast clear now. Sorry if I made you miss your train.'

'Three, actually. But I'll forgive you if the news is good.'

'I'm not sure I know what "good" is any more.'

Sonia accepted a glass of wine as she listened to the detail of the Timber Wolf meeting. 'So you reckon Gareth's definitely not fabricating but definitely is on the make? That must be fraud or theft. What do security think?'

'They don't know yet. They will tomorrow.'

'They're bound to want to consult the legal advisor and he's bound to say the police have to be told and sooner or later the story will come out that nasty Brits were spying on nice EU. You know what he's like.'

Charles knew only too well what his legal advisor was like, a paunchy, self-important man seconded from the Home Office who saw his job as primarily to stop people doing things. It had been hard enough getting him to put his stamp on the Tresco submission before it went into the Whitehall mill. Once he had his teeth into an issue like this he would be remorseless. There would be no end of complications, possibly even an inquiry into agent payments in general, which would rule that in future they had to be signed for by the agent in the presence of a visiting finance officer. Not to mention declaration to HMRC. He would probably also insist that security withdraw Gareth's vetting certificate, which was effectively to sack him since no one was allowed to work in SIS without one. 'Naturally, I don't want to tell anyone until we've decided whether or not we can exploit this in any way. But I need to get security on side.'

'Are you sure Gareth doesn't know you know about his keeping half the money?'

'He didn't show any sign of unease when I mentioned it. We'll have to assume that it will come out in some way if he talks enough to Timber Wolf. But that's all right. We might want him to carry on as he is.'

'Carry on?' It took a lot to surprise Sonia. 'Carry on with the case?'

'Yes, depending on what your Cheltenham friend can tell us. Have you got authority for what you want to do with them, by the way?'

'Almost.' She tried to hide her smile with her glass.

Charles looked at her, then let it go. 'We need to know of any contact between Gareth and Timber Wolf after my lunch in Brussels. They obviously were in contact but it would be useful to know who initiated it and whether there has been further contact since.'

'Bear in mind they might not be able to say what was said. Yet.'

'Also, anything they can produce on Timber Wolf's contact history before the lunch as well as after it. With people other than Gareth, I mean. Who did he talk to and when.'

'What exactly have you got in mind?'

'What I suspect you may already be thinking.' They looked at each other for several sedate ticks of the Cumming clock.

'You mean Timber Wolf might be a double agent, a DA?'

'Wouldn't it fit? Think about it. Someone is secretly working for you and shows a bit of skirt to the opposition. They take the bait and recruit him or her to be their secret agent – as they think. You give your agent plenty of chickenfeed to pass on, including some big stuff that you don't mind giving away because you know they know it anyway, or will find out. You let them have it a little bit in advance and they're delighted when they find it checks out. Adds verisimilitude, builds up your agent's credentials so that when you want them to swallow the big lie – as happened with the Double Cross system and the 1944 Normandy invasion – they do, hook, line and sinker.'

'But they haven't sold us any big lies. It all checks out.'

'That's the point. Adjust your prism and it all falls into place. As we well know and as you pointed out, Gareth and Timber Wolf have known each other for years, with Timber Wolf perfectly well aware that

Gareth was an MI6 officer under FCO cover. During all that time there was never a sniff of an intelligence relationship; Timber Wolf never volunteers a scrap of information about his EU Commission work. The Brexit referendum comes and goes and he still doesn't. Article 50 is triggered – still nothing. Then, when negotiations start, up he pops and says to Gareth, "Dear old friend, I am pro-British and can tell you things that would help Britain to get a good deal." Gareth takes the bait, offers him generous payments that Timber Wolf accepts without a qualm and goes on to provide intelligence at every meeting.'

'But he never asks for anything in return, never shows any curiosity about our own tactics, never tries to find out about our thinking, which is what a normal double agent would do.'

'Exactly. Because he's not a normal DA. They don't want to find out about us; they've no interest in laying false scents, as a normal DA might. They just want us to do something – up our offer. They let him tell us only what's true, nothing game-changing because they don't want the game to change. What he tells us adds flesh to what our negotiators see and hear across the table, including bits and pieces of titillating personal stuff about rows behind the scenes and so on, but never anything that alters the picture.'

'Until now. This revelation of the EU's real bottom line.'

'That's my point. They believe we're not going to up our

offer unless we're convinced they'll come part of the way to meet us. But no farther. So they slip the tasty morsel about their bottom line under the counter, prompting us – they hope – to up our offer without them having to say across the table that they're lowering theirs. Their aim is to persuade us that that's the only way to get a deal. And you can bet your bottom dollar that they then bag our offer, thank you very much, and go on bargaining for a little bit more, and a little more, and a little more, until we're close to what they've demanded all along. Or, if we refuse to keep upping our offer and threaten to walk away, they can simply accept the halfway house offer we've already been tricked into making. Which they might genuinely be prepared to accept anyway but they don't want us to know that because then we'd only offer half of a half, if you see what I mean.'

'So you think we should play it back at them?'

'Got it in one.'

'The FCO will never agree. Too risky, too complicated, too much smoke, too many mirrors.'

'But if we get it to the foreign secretary and the prime minister they might. Might. Politicians – even in this government – are generally less risk-averse than their officials.'

'But it's all surmise, Charles. Nice idea, has a logic of its own but it only works if your premise that it's a game being played against us is right, and you can't be certain of that. It's plausible, I agree, but it's still only surmise.'

'That's where Cheltenham can help. If you can get authority to put Timber Wolf properly on tap we might learn enough to be sure. It should be possible even with our own legal advisor involved now that we can truthfully argue that Timber Wolf could be a threat to British economic well-being. That's within the scope of our and Cheltenham's statute.'

'All right. But if we run it back at them, who runs it? You or Gareth?'

'Ideally Gareth. He has the established relationship. If we can get clearance for that. And if we can't, if he has notionally to go abroad or falls under a bus or whatever, I'll be his stand-in until he notionally returns. But that may raise suspicions, so it's better him.'

'Can you trust him? He's already shown you can't in the way he reports it and now with the money. He's a thief and if or when he comes to realise you know it—'

'And so long as I've done nothing about it I – we – have a hold over him. As for what we'd want him to feed back to them in terms of reactions here, he couldn't let us down because – so long as we brief him in such a way that he doesn't realise he's being briefed, letting things slip and so on – he wouldn't know he was being set up. If we can get clearance.'

Sonia raised her glass. 'If.'

*

He sensed something as he opened the front door that night. It wasn't just that Sarah was home – that he expected as he was later than usual – but he had a strong impression of something else, of another presence. There were no voices, no movements, but there was a tension in the silence. He paused on the doormat, still holding the door handle. Then he heard Sarah's quick step from the kitchen as she came round the staircase into the narrow hall. She paused, smiling but with her eyes fixed urgently on his as if willing him to something.

'Charles, hello,' she said brightly. She rarely used his name when they were alone. 'Guess who's here – Daniel.'

Daniel was sitting at the kitchen table wearing faded blue jeans and a heavy grey jumper frayed at the cuffs and flecked with white paint. He wore his scuffed brown working boots and had a tool-bag at his feet. His red hair and beard were tousled and dusty, as if he had been crawling through a cramped attic. He hadn't taken off his boots when he came into the house, a convention he had adopted since his conversion. He half rose when he saw Charles, smiling sheepishly and holding out a limp hand.

'Daniel – nice surprise, good to see you.' Charles felt he sounded unconvincingly hearty.

'Daniel's in a spot of bother,' said Sarah, speaking as if she were making an announcement on stage. 'He's come for a cup of tea and advice.' She had a glass of white wine before her.

'I'll have what you're having,' said Charles. He put his overnight bag in the hall and sat. 'Advice is the easy bit, at least for the advisor. What's the problem?'

Daniel looked solemn. 'The police have raided our house. They're still there. They walked in behind Akela when she got back from work. They said they don't need a search warrant if serious crime is suspected.'

'What serious crime? What are they looking for?'

'Me, among other things. They're taking knives from our cutlery drawer and are going through my tools.'

'But what's the crime— suspected crime? Haven't they said why?'

'I don't know. I only know what Akela said when she rang me while it was going on. They may have said now.'

'What about these knives? Nothing illegal, is there?'

'No. I bought some new knives recently from a street market in Victoria. I wasn't looking to buy any but they were reduced to almost nothing and they're good-quality Sheffield steel, hard to find now. Better than the usual Chinese stuff. I was actually there to get a new Stanley knife for work from the tool shop but I saw these and they were dirt cheap, going as a job lot – probably nicked – so I got them.' He smiled for the first time. 'I think Akela thought I was going on some murderous killing spree, like that bloke in Ely, though what I'd want with three carving knives and two bread knives when I've only got two hands I don't think she asked herself. But how did the police know about them? That's what worries me. I paid cash. Must have been the stallholder. Or are they following me? Would they do that?'

Charles nodded his thanks as Sarah poured his wine. It would not do to tell Daniel that his wife had been worried enough to voice concerns to her sister, who had told Sarah and Charles, who had told MI5, who must have told the police, who – without warning – had acted. 'What have they said to Akela?'

'Nothing much, nothing about the knives except that they went straight to the cutlery drawer and picked out the new ones and asked where we got them and whether she had any receipts and why we needed so many. They didn't find my Stanley knife because I've got it with me.'

'But it's you they're looking for?'

'Want to know where I am, when I'll be back, what I'm doing and all that. I think they must have taken her phone off her because she said she'd ring again, but she hasn't and I don't want to ring and put her in an awkward position.'

Charles didn't look at Sarah, conscious of the guilt she would be trying not to show and unwilling to risk reflecting it in his own expression.

'I came to you because – well, you're involved in

this sort of thing,' Daniel continued. 'And I wondered if you could – I don't know – sort of find out what's going on and tell them I'm a peaceful Muslim, not a terrorist.' He shook his head. 'I suppose it's all part of the so-called Prevent strategy, is it? Muslims only to be allowed forks and spoons.'

Charles spoke slowly, as a cover for thinking quickly. The trouble was, there wasn't much to think. The chief of MI6 had no executive authority outside MI6 itself, could not intervene in MI5 investigations and had no influence over or knowledge of police operations. Like any other British subject, he would be committing an offence himself if he helped a fugitive evade justice, even if he believed the fugitive innocent. 'Tell me exactly what Akela said they said. Did they say they want to arrest you or just question you?'

'I don't know. She just said they're looking for me.'

Charles knew from his own experience that police preferred to arrest if they could, rather than simply interview. Arrest – permissible if serious crime were suspected – meant they could search and interview under caution at times and places of their choosing, could record everything and use anything said as evidence. Arrest could be more convenient than inter-view, whether or not it was followed by a charge. 'The best thing,' he said, speaking with deliberation, 'for you and for Akela is to go home and hand yourself in. You've done nothing illegal, you've got nothing to worry about, they've not a shred of evidence against you and they can easily check with the street trader that the knives were a cheap job lot. If you go on the run they'll think you've something to hide and when eventually they find you – which they will – you'll have a much harder time convincing them of your innocence. And you'll make life more difficult for Akela, too. Not to mention your family. So long as you're missing they may want to search your mother's house, too.'

Sarah put her hand to her mouth. 'They wouldn't really want to bring Deborah into it, would they?'

'They'd question anyone thought to be close to Daniel.'

'What about you?' asked Daniel. 'Would they question you if they knew you'd seen me?'

'Quite likely, once they discovered our connection.'

'What would you tell them?'

Charles looked into Daniel's eyes. 'I'd tell them you'd been here, that I'd advised you to hand yourself in, that you had nothing to worry about because they were barking up the wrong tree and there was a perfectly innocent explanation for the knives.'

'Assuming that's all they're worried about.'

'Is there anything else they should be worrying about?'

Daniel looked down at his boots. The steel toecaps showed through the scuffing. 'I'm involved with a

Muslim charity that takes money and stuff out to Syria and places. They might suspect it raises funds for terrorists.'

'Does it?'

Daniel looked up. 'No.'

'Which charity?'

'I'd rather not say, if you don't mind. It's legal, it's registered with the Charity Commission and all that.'

'What do you do for them?'

'Anything I can. Driving, ferrying goods and people about, that sort of thing.'

There was a pause. Charles could sense Sarah's discomfort. He concentrated on Daniel. 'Best thing you can do, Daniel, is to go home now and get it over with. It won't take long and in a few days it'll be history. Ring the house from here, say you're on your way. Or we can do it for you.'

Daniel looked down at his boots again.

'Be prepared for them to ask you about more than just the knives. They'll probably ask about your friends and contacts, whether you know anyone with terrorist connections or extremist inclinations, that sort of thing. Again, play it straight and you've nothing to worry about.'

'You mean they'll try to get me to spy for them?'

'They might but not necessarily. If they do – well, it's up to you what you say. You don't have to, there's no compulsion, no coercion. Just be firm and polite. Always pays to be polite.'

'But isn't that what Prevent means? Penetrating Muslim communities and getting them to spy on each other? Getting teachers to spy on pupils?'

It was not the first time Charles had found himself having to defend, or at least account for, something in which he didn't believe. Prevent was almost a misnomer, chosen for alliterative reasons to go with Protect, Prepare and Pursue as part of the wider counter-terrorist CONTEST strategy. Never intended as a penetration operation, it was meant as a strategy to persuade vulnerable individuals away from violence or extremism by getting others in their communities to help. But making it a police responsibility like Pursue meant that many Muslims were reluctant to report friends or relatives for fear of arrest. Charles had argued that the attitudes needed to make it work had to arise from below, through day-to-day civic participation and trust in institutional fairness; anything enforced from above by official or officious interventions was likely to be counter-productive. Also not for the first time, he was grateful he was not running MI5 or the Met police.

'No, it isn't,' he said. 'We can talk about it another time if you like but it's irrelevant in your case, anyway.' He immediately regretted the phrase 'your case', with its implication that there might be a case to answer. 'All you need do is tell the truth and answer their questions politely. If you don't know something, just say so. And don't go beyond their questions, don't say more than necessary.'

'The landline's in the other room if you want to use it,' said Sarah.

Daniel remained silent for a few seconds, then shook his head as if in response to an internal dialogue. 'Thanks, I'll go now. Thanks for your help.'

When the door was closed and his footsteps had receded along Cowley Street, Sarah said, 'I knew it. I knew this would be a mess. We should never have got involved.'

'We didn't choose to be.'

'We didn't have to report what Anya told us. We could have just left it if there was an innocent explanation, as we now know there was. I wish I'd never spoken to that MI5 woman. Deborah's going to tear her hair out if – when – it gets back to her. D'you think they'll find out that we've been reporting?'

'There's no reason they should. Anyway, that's probably what Anya expected when she told us.' He was less sure about MI5 than he sounded. They should have informed him and Sarah before acting on their information.

'I'm inclined to ring that MI5 girl and give her a piece of my mind.'

'It's probably nothing to do with her, out of her hands. I'll ring Michael Dunton.'

Michael, whom Charles rang at home, knew nothing

about the police operation and promised to call back. He did so about forty minutes later. 'Apologies, Charles, apologies to you both. You're quite right that you should have been told. So should we. I've spoken to the head of SO15, the Met counter-terrorism bit, what we used to call Special Branch, and he didn't know about it either. It appears the decision was taken at lower level by a district commander without reference to anyone else. It's one of the drawbacks – one of not very many, I should say – of having the police embedded in our own CT section. Occasionally, one of them gets the bit between his teeth and charges off, thinking he's only doing what everyone wants. Generally, it's not like that – embedding works well to everyone's benefit – but this is one of the exceptions. I'm sorry. Please convey sincere apologies to Sarah. Apparently, they didn't find anything incriminating in the house search, though I think they took most of the cutlery drawer away. Can't think what good that will do them.'

'Daniel left here a while ago to hand himself in. At least, I think that's what he's doing. I've told him there's nothing to fear from talking to them.'

'Good. Let's hope he gets his knives and forks back.'

Chapter Ten

Robin Woodstock rested his elbows on his desk and put his two hands before him, palms together. He looked out of his window at St James's Park. The early-morning rain had eased but the plane trees still dripped and the runners skirted puddles. He looked back at Charles. 'Let me make sure I've got this straight before we talk to the foreign secretary. If we do.

'The EU official Timber Wolf and your number two, Gareth Horley, are old friends. They meet regularly over lunch and Timber Wolf passes information on EU thinking on the Brexit negotiations, which Horley reports as intelligence. The reports appear so far to be true and have been appreciated here. However, fearing that Horley may have exaggerated or even made up some of his reports, you have now met Timber Wolf. Your assessment was that Horley may have exaggerated or put words into Timber

Wolf's mouth but that he has not invented. You also discovered that Horley has been dishonestly pocketing half of the expenses he claimed to be paying Timber Wolf, who in fact has no expenses and clearly sees the money as payments for his information. You conclude that he sees himself as a paid agent of SIS, spying on his employers for us.

'Your suspicions were aroused by a recent report purporting to give the EU's secret fallback position on the so-called divorce settlement. You met Timber Wolf. When you asked him about this he was reluctant to name his sources or sub-sources. You concluded that although it is possible he is making the whole thing up, it is more likely that he was put up to it by the EU and is feeding us information in order to get us to increase our offer. Thus, the EU is using him as a double agent, pretending to be spying for us while in reality working for them. You believe this to have been the case from the start, that they tricked us into mounting an intelligence operation against them, something we would not otherwise have done and which would be a grave political embarrassment should they choose to reveal it. It could even bring down the government, given its small parliamentary majority. However, you also suspect that embarrassing us was not their aim in mounting the operation; that, you believe, was to persuade us to make the concessions they require.

'Given all this, you now propose that, instead of

breaking off the relationship, we turn it against them by using the untrustworthy but unsuspecting Horley to reveal that we have a secret divorce settlement ceiling significantly less than the minimum they demand but higher than what we have so far offered – which happens to be true – and that we would leave without a deal rather than exceed our secret ceiling. Which may or may not be true depending on the time of day and which minister we speak to.'

'But which is true of our own minister.'

'Probably true of the foreign secretary.'

'Whose authority we would need to do this.'

'Not only his.' Robin sighed and sat back, folding his arms. 'It won't surprise you to know it won't get my vote – too many ifs. But my worry is that he might rather like it. He's keen on doing things.' He emphasised the two last words. 'Appeals to his gung-ho side.'

'Is it time to go along to him?'

'I'll see if he's out of his shower.' Robin picked up his phone.

They had already been interrupted by the foreign secretary, shortly after Charles's arrival. He had appeared in Robin's doorway in shorts and running kit, wet and still slightly breathless. He had greeted Charles and then said to Robin, 'Got a moment when I've had my shower? That budget business. I've had an idea.' He turned again to Charles, who had stood. 'Business good? Plenty of spying? Bags of secrets for us?'

'Could be, Secretary of State, if you like what we've just been discussing.'

'Come along with Robin. Give me two ticks.' He ran his hand through his hair, showering the carpet with drips, and closed the door.

'Don't miss a bloody trick, do you?' said Robin.

Charles smiled and sat again. 'Not between friends. Anyway, whether we're to do it or not we need a decision today.'

'I must have something on paper.'

'That's in train now. It was mostly done last night. You'll get it in good time if he agrees.'

The foreign secretary, showered and now almost in suit and tie, was still perspiring slightly when they entered his office. He was the third foreign secretary Charles had worked for and so far there had been no disasters or difficult issues.

'Sit down, sit down.' The foreign secretary gestured as he tucked some of his shirt into his trousers. He looked at Charles. 'You run, don't you?'

'Just about. Not as far or as often as I should and slower than I used to.'

'Robin here doesn't believe in exercise. I keep telling him he should, take his mind off work, but he hates taking his mind off work and he stays thin.' The foreign secretary grabbed the flesh bulging through his shirt. 'Bloody annoying for someone like me. Now, have you got any goodies?'

'We've got a problem,' said Robin.

'Got enough of those already.'

'Which is also an opportunity,' said Charles.

'That's more like it.'

The explanation came mostly from Charles, with interjections from Robin, while the foreign secretary slumped expressionless on the sofa. As before when talking to this foreign secretary, Charles found himself talking too quickly, almost gabbling under the pressure of a quick and restless intelligence that had seen where he was going before he'd said it and was now on the brink of boredom, or had already moved on to something else. When he finished Robin added that, although there was nothing on paper yet, a submission was in preparation. He would make up his mind finally when he saw it in writing but meanwhile he would advise strongly against going along with what Charles proposed; there were too many risks, too many unknowns.

The foreign secretary, almost horizontal now, stretched his legs and pushed his fists into his trouser pockets. 'Tell me again exactly what you want to do,' he said to Charles.

'I'd like to let Gareth Horley continue with the case, at least for the time being. And I'd like to send him along to the next meeting primed with whatever we want the EU to believe we'd settle for, true or false.'

'But you just said this Howling Wolf or Jack

Russell or whatever you call him doesn't show any interest in finding out what we think but only tells us what they think, which is partly why you think it's a put-up job.'

'That's true but it's also possible that Gareth Horley is passing on gossip about our positions without declaring it. However, it could only be gossip because he's not au fait with the details of negotiations.'

'But you also said we can't trust him. So if we were to give him stuff to pass to them how could we trust him not to tell them that's what we were doing?'

'Because he wouldn't know. We'd engineer it in such a way that he came across something without knowing we wanted him to know it, contriving it so that he would think he'd found it out for himself.'

'Hard to control, isn't it? First you've got to make sure he finds out whatever it is without smelling a rat, then that he gets it right when he passes it on, then that he actually does pass it on, which he might well not and we would never know whether he had or hadn't. You wouldn't be able to ask him about it. Then, even if he does pass it on, you've got to trust your Springer Spaniel chappie to pick up on it and report it accurately. And we can't know about that, either.'

'Then there's the question of whether the other side believe it,' said Robin. 'We'd have no way of knowing.'

'Also, we'd have to get the prime minister's chop on it and I get the impression she's a touch more cautious than me.' The foreign secretary grinned. 'She's still sitting on that other submission of yours, the one about zapping that chap in Syria who's trying to get people back here to blow us all to smithereens.'

'And we'd have to decide in almost no time at all what the it – the "it" we want them to believe – actually is,' said Robin.

The foreign secretary shrugged. 'Not that difficult. We do exactly what they're trying to do with us, persuade them they've secretly discovered our absolute, irreducible, die-in-the-ditch bottom line. They want us to believe they'd settle for twenty per cent below their publicly stated figure but no lower, which is still way above what we would even consider. So we turn the tables. We convince them we'd go twenty per cent above our offer but not a centime more and that if we don't get it we'll walk away without a deal. Which is what I think we should do, anyway, but that's by the by. If we can get them to believe it –really believe it – they'll compromise. They always do, they're Europeans, they want to keep the show on the road. They suggest a figure halfway between the two that is more than I think we should pay but politically and economically we could live with it. It's high stakes but it's worth it so long as we're prepared to act as if we really will walk away, that we really mean it. That's where it might get difficult. In cabinet, I mean. But not all cabinet members need know about it.'

Charles felt it was going his way. 'D'you think the prime minister would agree?'

Grimacing, the foreign secretary took his hands from his pockets and ran them through his hair. 'Maybe. Probably. Possibly. Hard to say. She's met you, hasn't she?'

'In National Security Council meetings. We've had only one bilateral.'

'She might agree. Might.' The foreign secretary jerked himself upright, hands clasped before him, staring directly at Charles. 'Thing is – your crucial link, this Horley chap, is also your weak link. You admit you can't trust him so you have to find some complicated way of getting him to do it without realising he's doing it. Not a prospect guaranteed to win prime ministerial confidence. But what might work with her is if you do it yourself. You've met the Wolf chap, you got on with him, you reckon. If you can get him to take the bait in another meeting we'll at least know he's taken it and that it's the right bait. You become your own agent, as it were. What do you think, Robin?'

'Improvement of sorts, I suppose.'

Charles hesitated. The foreign secretary's stare was unyielding and calculating. 'Well, it could be me but it would surely be better, more natural—'

'I can see it might make for awkwardness with your Horley bloke when you hoof him off the case. But the whole thing is so chancy that it needs whatever level of reassurance we can give it. So that's the deal. It's that or no go.'

He was back in Head Office with minutes to spare before the monthly A&S – Admin and Support – meeting. He summoned Sonia to brief her on the revised submission.

'How do you think Gareth will take this?' she asked.

'Badly.'

'He might do something.'

'What d'you mean?'

'I don't know. I gather from a friend in HR that he's under more pressure about bullying, with a bit of groping thrown in now. Historic cases but more's coming to light. Can't be a very happy bunny. How much time do I have? When does the sub have to be over the river?'

'About ten minutes ago.'

'Thanks.'

He was tempted to delegate chairing the A&S meeting but he had done that the month before and was aware that he had a reputation for focusing on operational and Whitehall political matters at the expense of anything administrative and financial. It was another manifestation of what he now acknowledged to be a career-long professional failing and a lifelong character flaw: attending to what interested him and ignoring what didn't. Sarah, far more conscientious, pointed it out with increasing frequency. There had been periods in his career when personal preference and professional requirement coincided but as he became more senior they became less frequent. For the next hour, therefore, he strove to make amends by concentrating on BEE (Building Evacuation Exercise), HOSIP (Head Office Signage Installation Programme), on the venue for the APR (Annual Pensioners Reunion), on the monthly EDA (Equality and Diversity Assessment) and on the long-running issue of the provision of armoured cars for heads of station in dangerous parts of the world.

The latter had been running since well before he became chief and seemed likely to outlast him. Cath, director A&S, outlined progress since the last discussion. 'The MOD say that nothing, not even a tank, can be made fully bombproof but we know from work on ministerial and royal cars that worthwhile explosive mitigation and projectile resistance – blast and bulletproofing – can be installed on sound everyday vehicles. It wouldn't stop large bombs, of course, nor armour-piercing ammunition, but it's not bad with lesser stuff. The problem is, all the cars we use have to be UK-sourced. Made here, in other words.'

'Why is that a problem?' asked Charles.

'Well, as you know, CSS, most of our heads of station have diplomatic cover and therefore have to be seen to be driving British or British-made cars. It's a problem because when they're trying to blend in locally or do anything clandestine they don't want to use obviously British cars with diplomatic registrations. They want to use local cars with local registrations. In fact, they hardly ever use diplomatically registered cars, for obvious security reasons.'

'So what's the point in having them expensively armoured?'

'That's what they say. But the MOD will only armour cars made here because in order to do it properly they have to intervene in the manufacturing process. Also, there's another problem.' She paused to see that she had everyone's attention. 'The cars are intended only for stations at regular risk of terrorism – the Middle East, Cyprus, Islamabad, Kabul and so on – and the MOD doesn't want the materials and techniques they use to become known. Also, it's important that no one gets to the cars to bug or booby-trap them during production or en route. Therefore, they have to be flown out by RAF transport aircraft rather than commercial carriers. Now, if the cars are FAP – Fully Armour Protected – they weigh a lot more, heavier metal, glass, suspension, steering, everything. That means they weigh too much to go on standard RAF flights and have to be flown out by specially adapted planes at enormous expense. The alternative is PAP – Partially Armour Protected – which means that only the driver's window, door, floor and the windscreen are armoured. The stations say that's pointless because anyone can fire a bullet through any of the other windows.'

'They have a point, don't they?'

'But Marigold who does Health & Safety says it's better than nothing and it would cover our backs as far as they're concerned.'

'So it's really all about back-covering?'

'Well, no, not – I mean . . .'

Cath looked uncomfortable, glancing at the others in an appeal for support. Charles had no wish to make her suffer; it was not her fault that almost everything she had to do with exasperated him. 'But, leaving that aside,' he said, trying to sound conciliatory, 'would any of these vehicles, fully or partially armoured, withstand – say – a drone attack?'

Cath shook her head. 'No. Apparently even tanks won't.'

'What sort of cars are we talking about?'

'That's another problem. They're supposed to be grade-compatible, you see, appropriate to the FCO cover grade of the head of station, no ambassadorial limousines or anything. That means smaller eco-friendly engines, which aren't as powerful as bigger engines, and the two trial ones sent out to stations have been sent back as unusable.'

'Why?'

'Too heavy with the weight of armour. They won't go up hills.'

'Couldn't they have found that out before they sent them?'

'That's the MOD for you.' That at least brought smiles to the faces of the meeting. 'The thing is, CSS, we need a decision because if we're going to order any we have to do it before the end of this financial year.'

Bureaucratic decisions came easily to Charles, sometimes too easily; he could be flippant. He was anxious to bring the meeting to a close while trying not to make it too obvious. 'We say no, then. Tell the MOD that if they produce a car that is FAP, transportable, grade-compatible and goes up hills we'll look again at our decision.'

Cath looked surprised but not displeased. 'Well, yes, CSS, if you're – but there's still the question of H&S. Marigold has signed up to saying we've got to have them.'

'And so we shall, tell her, when they produce something that's fit for purpose.' That was a popular phrase with contemporary resonance. He had surprised himself by coming up with it. 'Must be FFP,' he added. 'And ask her to liaise closely with the MOD on lightweight materials research and possible drone countermeasures.' That should keep Marigold and her staff busy for the foreseeable future. 'Any other business?'

Stephen, Cath's youthful new deputy, a transferee from Work and Pensions, said that the report on the marauding exercise at Hyde Park that Charles had witnessed with Gareth Horley was still in draft. 'Main points?' asked Charles.

'The attack side of it went well. We estimate that, given seventy to eighty per cent building occupancy on the day, which is about normal for Head Office, there would have been between thirty and forty-five per cent casualties.'

'Alarm and evacuation procedures?'

'Not quite so well. Hence the casualties.'

'And the intervention force?'

'They achieved their object, which was to halt the attack. But they would also have caused quite a few of the casualties themselves, we think. And they would have suffered a few, which has H&S implications for future police deployment. The police aren't supposed to expose their staff to serious risk of harm without signed-off risk assessments. Which means we may not be able to call on them.'

'So who would we use?'

'The army, I suppose.'

'But they wouldn't be there.'

'No. Unless we knew about the attack in advance.'

'Bit of a shambles, then?' Charles smiled, to spare Stephen embarrassment. 'Useful because it proves what we've long suspected, so we can now make a case for better arrangements on the basis of evidence. No doubt the same would happen if there was an attack on this building now. Will the report suggest ways of improving our defences and procedures?'

Stephen made a note on his pad. 'I'm not sure. I'll ask.'

'Tell them if it doesn't, it must.' He looked around the room. 'Anything else?'

Eric, head of physical security, half-raised his hand. 'Just one thing, CSS. Not a big issue, or not yet. It's another of these LGBT – LGBT issues. I'm not sure whether now is the—'

'Don't worry, Eric, go on.' Eric was a lugubrious figure nearing retirement, not over-endowed with imagination or subtlety but solid and reliable. He was often uneasy in meetings and Lesbian, Gay and Transgender rights was a subject he found particularly awkward, shifting in his seat as he struggled with the conflict between his natural openness and a newly imposed bureaucratic culture.

'Well, it's – one of them, the latest person to declare that he or she is – is one of them, has said he or she – they – want their security pass to have two photos on it, one as a man, one as a woman, so that she – he – can choose whichever identity they want that day. We have had the same request before, once or twice, and we've said no but now I wonder – I don't know what the latest . . .'

Pauline, head of HR, turned to Charles. 'I think what's at stake here, CSS, is the question of whether the person's human rights are infringed by the denial of gender recognition, which would imply denial of gender choice.'

'What do the lawyers say?' No one knew. 'See that they're consulted, Pauline, and then we'll discuss again.' He turned to Eric. 'Thanks for raising it, Eric. Quite right to do so. Until we've had a chance to discuss again, carry on as you were.'

'Just say no?'

'Just say no.'

'There's also been a request from Stonewall,' continued Pauline. 'They've asked if we would like a representative on our board so that we can demonstrate that we're a fully inclusive employer. MI5 have one.'

'I think that's one for my successor,' said Charles. 'Whoever that may be.'

Back in his own office Jenny said that Michael Dunton wanted him to ring urgently on the secure line.

'He's disappeared, buggered off,' said Michael. 'Your young man, that is. You remember you said he was going home to hand himself in after leaving your place last night?'

'I thought that was what he was going to do – it was the impression he gave. It's what I advised him to do.'

'Well, he hasn't, I'm afraid, so there's now a hue and cry and his parents' place is being searched and her parents' place. The police will probably want to interview you and Sarah, too, since you seem to have been the last people to see him.'

Sarah rang a few minutes later. 'I've just had Deborah on the phone. The police are searching her house now, turning it upside down, taking her computer away and her mobile. She's distraught, she's had a great row with them and they've been really nasty, she says. She didn't even know Daniel was missing. She rang me to see if I could ask you to get them to call it off. I tried to tell her that you don't have that kind of authority but I think she thought I was just being unhelpful. I promised I'd speak to you and ring her back. What can I say?'

'Tell her there's nothing I can do and that we're in the same boat, almost. They'll probably want to interview us as we were the last to see him.'

'She'll want to know what he was doing at our house.'

'Tell her he came round for further discussion of the work he's supposed to do for us.'

'God, I wish we'd never – where on earth do you think he can be? Surely he's not about to go berserk in some crowded place, is he? Didn't he say they'd taken his knives away, anyway?'

'I've no idea what he's doing. Maybe he's run away to think about things. Or maybe he's trying to leave the country. Not to become a jihadi, necessarily, but maybe to join one of those Islamic aid charities.

He mentioned something about that, didn't he? But wouldn't say which. Just hope it's a good one, a real charity and not one that finances terrorism.'

'You really don't think he's a terrorist, then?'

Charles sighed. 'Well, he could be, of course. Anyone's capable of anything—'

'You believe they are? You really believe it?'

'Depending on context, yes.' In the pause that followed he sensed that he had unwittingly exposed a fissure between them, a fundamental disagreement about human nature, about what people were, that neither had suspected in the other. Now was not the time to explore it. 'But my feeling about Daniel is that he's not terrorist material, as I've said all along. He's enthusiastic for the cause and naïve about it, probably motivated by a strong sense of injustice and maybe, who knows, by some personal grievance.' Just like some of those who do become terrorists, he did not add.

'But where can he have gone? Akela must be worried sick. Quite apart from the hurt of being left like that, without a word.'

Jenny hovered in the doorway. 'I'll let you know if I hear more,' said Charles. 'Meanwhile, tell Deborah we're doing everything we can. Which is little enough but we'll keep her informed.'

'Sonia,' said Jenny as he put down the phone. 'Wants to talk urgently.'

'Show her in.'

Sonia clutched a clipboard to her breast and looked tense. She shut the door behind her. 'He's gone,' she said.

Charles hesitated. 'How do you know?'

'His wife rang in this morning.'

'Wait a minute. Who's gone?'

'Gareth, Gareth Horley. Whom d'you think I meant?' She sat. 'Missing, I mean. Gone missing. Can't be found.'

'Hasn't turned up for work?'

'Nor at home. His wife rang in this morning, as I said. He didn't come home from work last night and she thought there must be some urgent travel he hadn't told her about – which has happened before, apparently – but when he didn't turn up this morning or send any messages she rang the office. His assistants say he left yesterday afternoon a bit early for him and without saying where he was going. Security pass records show him swiping out at 4.53. Since then nothing. He's not answering either his office or his personal mobiles and their location trackers are switched off. Nor is he responding to emails. Suzanne, his wife – I haven't spoken to her myself – is desperate, apparently. Fears he may have thrown himself into the Thames. She says he's been anxious and tense recently, uncommunicative.'

Charles glanced towards the river. 'If he's gone in there it won't be long before we see him again.'

'What do you mean?'

'A river policeman told me that bodies go out with the tide and are brought nine-tenths of the way back by the next incoming tide. So it takes a long time to leave the river.'

Sonia stared. 'Cool, Charles, bordering on frigid, even by your standards. No matter what he's done, he was your friend, wasn't he? Not to mention possible successor.'

'I'm only saying it because I can't believe that's what he's done. Gareth goes for things, he doesn't run away from them. If he's gone into hiding it will be to do something, not to end it all.'

'Such as?'

'No idea.' They both paused. 'Is his passport . . . ?'

'In his safe in his office, where he always keeps it in case of urgent travel. Ditto overnight bag with spare clothes, shaving kit and so on. No one's checked his credit card yet nor got on to Cheltenham to see if they can locate his phones. His car is at home, ditto Suzanne's.'

'Alias passports?'

'He has two, according to Docs & Ids – Documents and Identities. Used to have more, of course, when natural-cover ops were more feasible than now. Ditto driving licences, bank cards and all the other alias paraphernalia. His secretary – sorry, assistant – is searching for them at the moment.'

'Have you done the submission?'

'I sent it to you twenty minutes ago. Suppose I'll have to redo it now to include this latest development. We can't very well not tell them, can we? Officials will be even less keen regardless of what the foreign secretary thinks. Won't go down very well with the PM, either, I'd have thought.'

Charles nodded.

Sonia sighed. 'I mean, for all we know he could be holed up with some journalist somewhere who's about to blow the whole story and bring the negotiations crashing down.'

'Why would he want to do that?'

'To get his revenge in first. That's the kind of man he is, I've always thought. I know you haven't.' She shrugged. 'But they ought to know, oughtn't they, in Whitehall? We can't not tell them.'

'They ought, yes.' Charles looked again in the direction of the river. Most of it was blocked from sight from Smith Square but there was a sliver just visible between St. John's and the buildings on the Embankment. Life would be simpler if Gareth took that option. But he wouldn't, he was sure. He'd have an agenda and somewhere, somehow he'd be pursuing it. It would no longer include rising to the top of the Service, of course, nor any other Whitehall plum. He'd burned his boats now. Maybe something financial, somewhere abroad. 'But later,' he continued, 'we'll tell them later. Important thing now is to get the EU negotiators to believe what we want them to believe. Which means getting the sub signed off a.s.a.p.'

'Shouldn't take long if the foreign secretary's already agreed in principle.'

'The PM hasn't, nor the Brexit secretary, who doesn't yet know about it. You know as well as I do that in Whitehall if it's not on paper it doesn't exist. So better get it over.'

'You haven't read it yet.'

'I've learned to trust your drafting over the years. Now find Gareth.'

'Is that all?'

As Sonia left Jenny again poked her head around the door. 'Suzanne Horley has been ringing you. Wants you to call her back. I've got their home number here.'

Perhaps a body had been found after all. However, Suzanne sounded self-possessed and matter-of-fact. 'I suppose you know what's happened?'

'I know Gareth's disappeared, yes. Is there anything . . . ?'

'No news, nothing at all. I suspect he has another woman somewhere. He must have – he wouldn't run off to commune with himself in solitude. You don't know of any mistresses, Charles? Be honest, we've all known each other long enough and I've no illusions about Gareth. It's a feature of our marriage. Has been for years.'

It was true that Gareth had long had a reputation for what was jocularly referred to as playing away from home. Charles, like others, had accepted it with a mental shrug; so long as it didn't impinge on the job it was Gareth's business. Tough on Suzanne, of course, lovely woman like that, hard to see why he'd want to hang up his cap elsewhere but there you are, needs must. Not the only chap who can't keep his flies done up, has to follow where the compass needle points. Such had been the attitude of most of Gareth's male colleagues, Charles included when he bothered to think about it, which was rarely. Listening to Suzanne now and wondering again whether morality might be indivisible after all, he was reminded of his own complacency. But there was no time for introspection and to tell her about the Brussels mistress, identified via the call-data on Timber Wolf's phone, would technically be a crime. He opted for the lie by omission. 'He's never confided anything about his personal life to me, nor anything about your marriage. What I'm thinking we might have to do if he doesn't turn up very soon is to ask MI5 to investigate him. What he carries in his head would constitute a major security breach if it all came out – virtually all our significant operations. I have a responsibility to report to MI5 anything that falls within their national security remit, as this plainly does. The advantage from your point of view is that with the technical resources at their disposal they're more likely to find out pretty quickly where he is than anyone else.'

'You don't think I should report him to the police as a missing person?'

'You could but it's early days and it may take a while to interest them. If you have a joint account, though, it would be worth checking it for unusual withdrawals. And let me know.'

'Good idea, yes, I'll do that.' She paused. When she spoke again her voice had lost its crispness. 'It's just been such a ... I don't really know how to describe it, it's such a shock and yet I'm not surprised. It's as if I've been half-expecting it. And you've been a good friend to Gareth over the years – and now Sarah as well, of course – you must feel let down just as I am. Not to mention the boys, who don't know anything about it yet. I can't think what I'm going to say to them. And then there's our other friends, people like the Ruttes – they're a Dutch couple we were friendly with in Geneva. Gareth's seen a bit of Eddie again recently and there's talk of a family holiday together. I don't know how I'm going to break it to them.'

Charles didn't want to discuss Timber Wolf. 'Let's just wait and see. There may be no news to break. He may surprise us all by turning up tonight.'

He next summoned Alex, director of security over-all. Alex was Eric's boss and, like Eric, was due to retire. He was a cheerful Scot with a ruddy farmer's face. Nothing seemed to surprise him and he sustained his good cheer despite a daily diet of problems. 'There's something you need to know, Alex, which no one else needs to know. In fact, it's very necessary that no one should know.' He indoctrinated him into the Timber Wolf case and told him everything about Gareth, except the plan to continue the case himself.

'So he's just disappeared, vanished completely? No note, no message, no communication at all? Sure he hasn't gone under a bus? Worth checking with police and hospitals. It happens all the time.'

'Of course, we'll have to do all that but you might have expected Suzanne to have heard something by now if that had been the case. Our priority, apart from finding him, is to establish whether he's blown the Timber Wolf case or any of the many other cases he knows, whether he's involved with anything more serious than the expenses fiddle we now know about and to get MI5 to agree to open an investigation, which will mean suspending him to start with.'

'HR will say that employment law says you can't suspend anyone without telling them and giving them reasons. And in this case there's no one to tell.'

'But you can withdraw his vetting clearance and cancel his pass, can't you? No one's allowed to work here without vetting or allowed in the building without a valid pass. As soon as you do that he's effectively suspended. On full pay. We'll go on paying him while he's investigated as a security risk. It buys us time for MI5 to do a proper job, assuming we haven't found out what he's up to in the meantime.'

'I'll set the wheels in motion.'

Charles knew what it was like when the power of the state turned against you, ineluctable and as impersonal as the sea. Within minutes Gareth would be transformed from insider to outsider, from being an enabler of state power to the object of it, a case for investigation. Conceivably, he could be exonerated and unexpectedly rewarded, as Charles had been; more likely, he would be subjected to due process and afterwards neither victimised nor further punished, merely excluded. And for those who aspired to do the state some service, exclusion was the deepest and most lasting punishment.

That evening, in Downing Street, he sat in the cabinet room overlooking the garden with the foreign secretary, the Brexit secretary and the prime minister's private secretary. A larger meeting had just finished and the atmosphere in the room still resonated with bodies, speech and movement. The two politicians were relaxed, the Brexit secretary leaning back in his chair, hands in pockets, retailing an anecdote about someone in Brussels. The foreign secretary nodded and smiled while looking at his phone. 'His statement here says precisely the opposite,' he said.

The Brexit secretary guffawed. 'Course it does. What do you expect? That's why he's called Both Ways.'

The private secretary, seated a discreet two places apart from the politicians, smiled and said nothing. He was a slim, bespectacled, alarmingly youthful-looking man whose expression suggested alertness and self-restraint. Charles had known him off and on for some years, initially as a promising young MOD official with nuclear expertise. He sat with pen and notepad before him.

'Point of this meeting,' said the foreign secretary, 'is to get absolutely clear what you're going to say to your lupine friend when you meet him. The PM has agreed your submission without demur – correct, Simon?' The private secretary nodded. 'But insists that what our lupine friend thinks he wheedles out of you must be word for word, syllable by syllable, what our battling negotiators here want the other side to understand about our position. Which happens to be the truth. We're not selling them a pup but trying to persuade them to recognise reality. So far, it's like dealing with a pack of religious nutters. They're fixated on maintaining the political purity of the EU project rather than trying to work out what works best for everyone. Next round of talks starts on Wednesday. Can you meet your lupine friend before that?'

'We're lunching on Monday.'

'Good for you. Great tradition, the Brussels lunch.' The foreign secretary gave a conspiratorial grin. 'You arranged it before you knew the submission was agreed, then?'

'The precautionary principle.'

'Your man Horley,' said the Brexit secretary. 'How's he taking this?'

'His vetting certificate has been withdrawn and he's been suspended pending investigation. He no longer has access to the case nor to anything else.'

'But how's he taking it?' The Brexit secretary's manner was still relaxed but his gaze was calculating. 'Not likely to run off to the press and spill the beans, is he?'

Charles had to make his own calculation. If he told them about Gareth's disappearance the submission would have to be redrafted and resubmitted with a strengthened risk assessment, which would mean it was less likely to obtain the prime minister's agreement. At the same time, all concerned – prime minister included – wanted the operation to go ahead. If it contributed even in a small way to a reasonable settlement, it was in the national interest that it should do so. If, meanwhile, Gareth intended to expose all in the press or on the web then the damage would be done whether or not Charles's lunch with Timber Wolf happened. But Charles felt Gareth would not blow everything, or not yet. Whatever hidden bitterness he might feel towards the Office or Charles personally, he would surely be reluctant to expose his old friend Timber Wolf. So Charles hoped.

'We've no evidence so far that he's in that frame of mind,' he said.

The Brexit secretary's gaze continued. 'You're keeping an eye on him?'

'We're involving MI5.'

'Now the message, the message you've got to get over,' said the foreign secretary, 'is essentially this: that the absolute max we'll pay for the so-called divorce settlement is twenty per cent above the figure that's in the public domain as our max. That's a significant concession, large enough to create political difficulties here but manageable. Not a penny more. That would be politically and publicly unacceptable. Second thing you've got to get over is that if the trade negotiations don't yield a deal that's reasonable for both sides, then we'll walk away, taking our divorce payment with us. You may not hear the prime minister repeat in public that no deal is better than a bad deal but that's still our position. Nothing is agreed until everything is agreed, remember. We really will walk away and they've got to be made to believe it, which they don't yet. Preparations for no deal are in progress. Simon here has a note of the precise form of words the prime minister wants put over.'

The private secretary read aloud a few sentences

from his notebook. It sounded like a list of abbreviated bullet points. Listening and at the same time considering how to put it over reminded Charles of his recent telephone conversation with Timber Wolf, setting up the Monday lunch. He had rung him in his office, something he would never normally do with an agent, but it was in keeping with the fiction that neither had anything to hide.

'Just wanted to update you on Gareth,' he had said, introducing himself by his first name only. 'He's back from his travels but unfortunately he seems to have brought back some pretty nasty disease with him, something he must have picked up. He's having tests for tropical diseases but asked me to let you know, to send his very best wishes and to say that he looks forward to resuming your lunches soon.'

There was the slightest hesitation before Timber Wolf expressed conventional considerations and concern, adding, 'This is indeed unfortunate. I was hoping he would have time for another lunch before the talks I am involved in resume next week. After that it will be much busier and I may find it difficult to meet.'

'No chance, I'm afraid. He'll be out of action for some weeks at least. But if you're genuinely at a loose end meanwhile, I'm in Brussels for a Monday-morning meeting and might be able to get away in time for lunch.'

There was another slight pause. 'If you are able to do

that it would be very nice to see you, Charles. Perhaps I can give you a little present to take back to Gareth.'

Simon read through the bullet points again, slowly. 'There's a copy for you.' He pushed a plain sheet of A4 paper along the polished cabinet table. The list was double-spaced, with no heading and no security classification.

'It's very important that the message he takes away is exactly that wording,' said the foreign secretary. 'Not the easiest thing to convey naturally between mouthfuls, unless your conversations are usually abbreviations.'

'Oscar kilo.'

Chapter Eleven

The following morning, Saturday, there was a knock on the door in Cowley Street a little after eight. Sarah was in the bathroom and Charles was dressed and getting breakfast. He approached the door teapot in hand, remembering just in time to look through the spyhole. He remembered, too, that the security inspection of their house – now mandatory for anyone in his position – had recommended the fitting at public expense of a reinforced door, steel bars on the windows, extra locks and a CCTV camera outside. It was another bit of admin he had done nothing about. The spyhole was there when they bought the house.

It showed Anya, Daniel's sister-in-law, wearing jeans and a padded jacket and holding a bicycle. She was gushingly apologetic. 'I am so sorry, Sir Thoroughgood—'

'Charles.'

'Sir Charles—'

'Not sir at all, I'm not one, just Charles. Come in. Have you had breakfast?'

'Thank you, yes, I don't want to intrude, really I don't need any breakfast. It's just that I have a message from my sister which she didn't want to trust to the telephone.'

'Please come in, you can chain your bike to the railings.'

'It's not my bike and I've forgotten the chain.'

'Bring it into the hall, then.'

By the time they had sorted it out Sarah was downstairs. 'Anya, how nice to see you. Come and sit down.'

'No, please, I mustn't interrupt your breakfast.'

'You'll only be interrupting if you refuse to sit down with us. Come on.'

Despite having declined breakfast, she sipped tea and nibbled a piece of toast. Her message from Akela was a question: what would happen to Daniel if he handed himself in now? Would he be arrested or charged? If so, with what? They patted the subject to and fro across the table, like gentle warm-up table tennis. Charles and Sarah tried to be reassuring without really knowing the facts. They thought he might be arrested and would certainly be questioned but, having done nothing for which he could be charged, that should be all.

'He's done nothing at all, has he?' asked Sarah. 'Unless you and Akela know anything different?'

Anya pushed her hair from her face. 'No, he hasn't done anything except run away. At least, so far as I know. He must think he's in trouble for converting to Islam and buying those knives. But now that he's run away the police will think he's hiding something and that makes it worse.'

'Not if he gives himself up,' said Charles. 'Much better than being caught.'

'How is Akela?' asked Sarah.

'She is calm, quite calm. She is taking it very well.'

'Does she know where Daniel is?'

'No, of course not. Otherwise she wouldn't be so worried.'

'But it sounds as if she isn't really very worried,' continued Sarah. 'Not about what's happened to him. She's more worried about what might happen to him if he's arrested. Which suggests that she might perhaps know where he is.'

Anya carefully lowered her cup to the saucer and pushed back her hair again. 'Well, I hadn't thought of that. She has not said anything to me to suggest she knows.'

'Would she like it if I came back with you to see her, to talk to her?'

Anya looked up. 'If you could, yes, I am sure. But wouldn't it – mightn't it get you into trouble?'

Sarah turned to Charles, who shrugged. 'It's not Akela who's under suspicion. It's a perfectly laudable aim, trying to persuade her to persuade Daniel to give himself up. Assuming she knows where he is or is in contact with him.'

'What will the police say about it if they question us?'

'They should be grateful. Should be. I'd have thought.'

Sarah turned to Anya. 'It would be better if you were there. Shall I come back with you now?'

'Yes, yes, but I have my bike.'

'Leave it here and I'll drive you back to pick it up later.'

Charles cleared the breakfast table while Anya went to the loo and Sarah went upstairs for her coat. 'You don't mind, do you?' she whispered when she came down. 'It won't make things awkward to have me intervening?'

'An inspired thought. You might be right. Akela might know something.'

'Inspired mainly by the hope of keeping Deborah off my back, if I'm honest.'

Charles walked across Smith Square to Head Office. Intelligence services functioned twenty-four hours a day throughout the year but unless there was an emergency their routines were pretty much nine-to-five, like the rest of public service. A few people would be in, catching up or responding to some local incident in Kabul or Mexico City or wherever. Apart from them it would be just the duty officer and a few – probably too few – guards. The one who greeted Charles had been in the Service at least as long as himself, an over-weight, unsmiling man with an occasional flicker of morose humour.

'Morning, sir. She's beaten you to it.'

'Who's beaten me to what?'

'Your lady-friend, your fellow conspirator. Arrived ten minutes ago.'

It could only be Sonia. Not for the first time, Charles marvelled at how much was known by ancillary staff. He should have realised. The Service had recruited them as agents often enough. Cleaners, guards, drivers, maintenance staff, cooks, window-cleaners, babysitters – especially babysitters – often had free access and a good idea of who came and went, when, where and with whom. He remembered the case of a dockyard laundryman who provided accurate and up-to-the-minute intelligence about the destinations and durations of warships and submarines.

He turned on his screen before ringing Sonia. The first item was a message the previous evening from Michael Dunton to the effect that police were about to arrest members of Daniel's mosque committee and possibly also Akela. He rang Sarah but there was no answer; her Golf was not fitted with hands-free tech-nology. He left a message summarising Michael's and then rang Sonia.

She came to his office with a mug of mint tea and her usual clipboard. 'What are you doing here?' Charles asked. 'The submission is cleared. You didn't need to spend another weekend working. Are you just catching up on the day job?'

'Working out where Gareth Horley might be. Much more interesting.'

'And where's that?'

'Brussels. Possibly staying with Timber Wolf, or hidden by him. But more likely with his mistress since he doesn't know we know about her.'

'You didn't need to come in to conclude that. It's what I've been thinking, too.'

'But I did need to come in to check passenger lists.'

'How? We don't have access—'

'MI5 and GCHQ do, where there's justifiable national security interest.' She put her tea on his desk and sat. 'Fortunately, my contacts with both continue to prove helpful.'

'More so than mine at the moment.'

'That's because you operate at too high a level. Down at desk level people know things and can do things.' She opened her clipboard. 'Mr Rodney Rushlake to the Eurostar to Brussels on Wednesday evening. Single, just hand baggage. That's one of Gareth's old aliases for which he still has documentation.'

'I thought once they were closed we no longer had any docs or any record of them.'

'We don't but MI5 do. When they were created we used to log them with MI5 and they logged theirs with us in case two people were issued with the same one. They keep better records than us. We have Mr Rushlake logged as closed but it never was. They have it as still open, complete with bank account, credit cards, driving licence, passport, the full hand. It appears that Mr Horley has kept Mr Rushlake alive for years in case of need, which suggests a long-term criminal cast of mind, if not of actual intent. We can close all the accounts and cancel the passport with a telephone call. And do the same with another of his aliases, which we also had logged as closed and which is still extant. He's probably got all that documentation with him as a standby. If we closed both down he'd be helpless, unable to travel anywhere or pay for anything.'

Charles again tried to reconcile the Gareth he thought he knew with the Gareth who was now emerging. He must indeed have had a criminal cast of mind, as she called it. Necessary, perhaps, for a good operational officer; you needed guile, a willingness to bend or break rules, an eye for the main chance and a fallback, always a fallback. At least one. But you needed integrity, too, honesty and the self-discipline to use criminal tactics for good ends only. Perhaps a less common combination than Charles had assumed. 'But if we closed them down he'd know, wouldn't he? Know we were on to him.'

'Would that matter? Once he knows he's isolated and virtually helpless wouldn't he be more likely to give himself up?'

'But do we want him to? He might be more useful where he is.' He told her what had been agreed in Number Ten the previous evening.

'If you're to be the message-bearer, what role can there be for him?' she asked. 'Whitehall wouldn't want him involved because they know from us that he can't be trusted. Quite rightly. That's why they want you – you just said.'

'But it may be helpful if he has an unconscious supporting role. Essential that he doesn't know it, of course. If he is in Brussels and if this is an EU intelligence operation, as we suspect – albeit an ad hoc one because they don't have any operational intelligence capacity, as yet – then they'll want to debrief him, won't they? A renegade intelligence officer who has burned his boats and has nowhere to hide unless they find him a home and who is sympathetic to their cause – how could they resist debriefing him themselves, or at the very least doing it via Timber Wolf? It's therefore essential that he and Timber Wolf do not give contradictory accounts.'

'But that would mean you'd have to see him.'

'It would.'

'And Whitehall wouldn't like you involving him.'

'If they knew.'

They looked at each other in silence. 'New territory for me,' she said. 'Too political, deceiving our masters.'

'And for me.'

'Not sure I believe that.'

Charles wasn't sure he did, either, though he couldn't remember contemplating anything quite like this before. It didn't feel different from everyday espionage, merely like an extension of it. 'If I could find him – big if – I'd have to convince him I'd come to persuade him to come back and resign honourably, nervous breakdown, medical retirement, that sort of thing. And in the process I'd let slip what I had already let slip to Timber Wolf. Then, when I'd failed to persuade him to come home – essential that I did fail – he and Timber Wolf would sing from the same hymn sheet to their EU masters.'

'Mightn't you be conniving with criminality?'

'Maybe. Talking of which, any chance you could ask your helpful contacts whether the names Daniel Adamson or Abdul Salaam Adamson come up on any of their travel lists?'

'Who are they?'

'He is Sarah's Muslim convert godson who's gone missing. He's wanted by the police, though as far as we know he hasn't actually done anything except buy a few knives and have friends they're worried about. MI5 know all about it. That's how we come to be involved.'

'He'll already be on stop lists, presumably, which

means there's nothing more we can do.' She smiled. 'Even if I were to sully my professional hands with a sordid private initiative.'

'I had a message from the DG about him only this morning. We've been reporting on him to MI5 but we've no idea – certainly no influence over – what's going on at working level. It's making life very awkward for Sarah. She's probably with his wife now.'

Sonia stood. 'I'll let you know if I pick up anything.'

She rang ten minutes later. 'A little bird tells me they've arrested some of his friends and are searching his house again. But you'll know that from Sarah, I assume?'

Charles rang Sarah's mobile but there was again no reply.

Sarah spoke with deliberation, ignoring her phone and trying not to sound exasperated. 'But we're not asking to go in,' she said again to the policewoman, resting her hand on Anya's shoulder. 'This is Mrs Adamson's sister. She'd like to speak to Mrs Adamson. There's no harm in that is there, if Mrs Adamson is not under arrest?'

The policewoman was pale and unsmiling. She looked as if she'd been up all night. 'The property is being searched as a potential crime scene and no one is allowed in. I must ask you to move on.'

She too was repeating herself, standing just inside the blue and white tape that extended from the door of the terraced house, across the pavement, around Daniel's small Vauxhall van and back to the door of the next house. A police car and Transit van were parked on the far side of the road and a policeman was directing traffic through the narrow gap. Passers-by stared but no one lingered.

Anya leaned across the tape towards the policewoman. 'Please, this is ridiculous. If my sister is not under arrest, why may I not speak to her? I don't have to go in; she can come out. I only want to know how she is, if she's all right.'

'I'm sorry, madam, I must ask you to move on.'

'But why are you here? What is all this for? The house has already been searched. You know her husband is not here. She does not know where he is. Why are you bothering her again?'

The policewoman turned her back.

Sarah nodded to Anya to move away. 'Try ringing her again,' she said quietly. 'The house phone this time. If she knows we're here she might come out. Presumably they can't stop her, unless she is actually under arrest.'

The phone was answered immediately and Anya spoke rapidly in Urdu. She stopped, listened, began again, then stopped once more. She held the phone before her, looking at it. 'They've cut her off.'

'What did she say?'

'She said she has been arrested on suspicion of aiding and abetting— look, here she is, she's coming out.'

A policeman led the way across the pavement, followed by Akela and another policewoman. Akela was not handcuffed but looked shocked and subdued. Anya went back to the tape and leaned across it again, calling out to her sister. The policewoman turned and raised her hands in front of Anya's face. 'Madam, please stand back. Stand back!' Another policeman emerged from the house and stepped across to support his colleague. Another lifted the tape for Akela to duck beneath on her way to the police car, but before she did so she turned towards Anya and Sarah, speaking rapidly. Anya asked a question, which Akela was still answering as the escorting policewoman put her hand on the top of her head to guide her into the car.

When it had driven off Anya turned away, whispering, 'She told me. Where Daniel is. She just told me. She wants us to see him and tell him what has happened.'

'Where is he?'

'Penhurst Road, number twenty-three. It's near here. She said it's an empty house he has been working on. The owners are away and left him the key. Shall we see him now?'

Sarah hesitated. They were walking quickly back towards her car, parked illegally at the bottom of the street. Would this constitute aiding and abetting a fugitive? Whether it did or not, what consequences might it have for Charles, given his position? Or for herself. It was not the kind of publicity her law firm would relish. She realised only at that moment that thinking of Charles first had become a habit. They were in her car before she replied. 'So long as our intention is to persuade him to give himself up I suppose it might be justifiable.'

'That's what we can say, anyway.'

'If he won't our legal obligation is to report his whereabouts to the police.'

Anya laughed. 'We're not going to worry too much about that, are we? Unless we find him planning some outrage, which I can't believe. Does your satnav work? She said it's near here.'

It was a terraced house similar to Daniel's but bigger. Sarah knew the layout without seeing it: a hall with stairs leading away from the front door, two rooms on the right probably knocked into one, a kitchen at the back now extended into a utility room and loo, three bedrooms and a bathroom upstairs. To the front was a small low-walled garden featuring two plastic dustbins and an untidy privet hedge. On the road outside was a builder's skip filled with rubble, discarded doors and floorboards. The windows were too dusty to see through.

Anya had to ring twice before the door opened.

Daniel stepped back, holding it at arm's length so that he was barely visible from the road. They slipped in without saying anything.

'Akela told you?' Daniel asked when he had closed the door. He wore the same dusty jeans and paint-flecked jumper as when Sarah had last seen him.

'Yes, as she was being taken away.' Anya described what had happened as they walked through to the kitchen, where the sink, cupboards, work surface and units were half-assembled. They had to pick their way through the tools on the floor. Daniel cleared some screws from the small table and gestured to them to sit.

He looked at Sarah. 'Why have they arrested her? What's the point?'

'I don't know. I don't know whether she's actually under arrest or whether they've just asked her to go and be interviewed at the police station. She wasn't handcuffed or anything but they've taken her mobile and seem to be searching your house again.'

'They won't find anything there.'

'Nor anywhere else?' She said it as gently and unprovokingly as she could.

He turned to her, holding the kettle he was about to fill. 'The trouble with people like you, people like you and Charles, is that because you don't believe in anything yourselves you can't understand people who do. I'm not a terrorist, I worship Allah. Islam is a religion of peace, that's what the word means. Becoming a Muslim doesn't mean becoming a terrorist. Nor does the fact that I'm helping – going to help – with charity work for suffering Muslims in the Middle East mean that I'm a jihadi.'

Sarah waited while he filled the kettle. 'I believe you, Daniel, but I wanted to ask because it's the kind of question the police will ask when they— when you decide to talk to them. They're bound to ask how you intend to help in this charity work, which charities and so on. They'll also ask about your Muslim friends. You have to—'

'Get my story straight?'

'Be clear and honest and don't overreact.'

He continued to look at her as he held the kettle. 'I don't think I've overreacted.'

'I'm not saying you have.'

'But they have. There's no reason for arresting Akela, none at all.'

'I agree. Certainly none that I can think of.'

'Why have they, then?'

'Maybe it's just because they can't find you. Maybe they think she knows where you are.'

'Will she be in trouble?'

'She could be, if she's found to be aiding and abetting a fugitive.'

'So you think I should give myself up? Is that what you're saying?'

'That's why we came here,' said Anya. 'That's what we came to tell you.'

Daniel plugged the kettle into a socket that hung by its wires from the wall, pulling a chair across to rest it on. 'I can't understand why they're so desperate to talk to me. I don't know anything, I haven't done anything, I'm not planning to do anything.'

'I suspect it's not so much you as some of the people you're associating with,' said Sarah. 'Is it possible that one or two of them have dodgy records?'

'I don't know about the past. One of them was in Guantanamo but none of them has ever said anything to me about becoming a terrorist.'

'And what about your charity work? Are they involved in that?'

'Not really. One of them put me in touch with the charity I'm helping.'

'What kind of charity?'

'Aid, supplies, what you'd expect. Not so much medical and foodstuffs as communications equipment, water sterilisation kits, that sort of thing.'

'What will you do for them, raise money or buy supplies or ... ?'

'Nothing much, just manual work, help load stuff, drive stuff, that sort of thing. Only for a few days, that's all.'

'Where?'

'Why are you asking all these questions? Nothing wrong with it, is there? Nothing illegal? Are you going to try and stop me?' He reached for the kettle as it switched itself off, staring at Sarah with burgeoning hostility.

'No, Daniel, I'm just asking the kind of questions the police will probably ask. They'll want to satisfy themselves that you're not planning anything. That doesn't mean they think you are.' She wasn't at all sure about that. 'Anyway, as I said, I don't think it's really you they're interested in.'

'I'm not going to inform on fellow Muslims, if that's what they're thinking.'

'I don't suppose they are, not for a moment.' She was even less sure of that. 'My – our – point is that it's better to hand yourself in and get it over with than wait until they find you. Better for you, better for Akela. Also, if you're thinking of going abroad with this charity you'll probably get picked up at the airport and prevented from leaving. Or you'll get picked up on the way back like all these returnees from Syria they're always looking out for.'

Daniel shook his head. 'There are ways.'

'Think of Akela,' said Anya. 'She must be terrified and worried sick about what's going to happen to you when they find you. At least if you hand yourself in she won't be in any danger and she'll know you're all right.'

'Assuming I would be.'

'They're not exactly going to send you to Guantanamo.'

'They might. They might send me down for

twenty-five years just for being in the wrong place at the wrong time. That's what happened to my friend who was sent to Guantanamo. He was picked up in Afghanistan where he was doing charity work.'

Sarah assumed this was the man the MI5 desk officer, Shelley, had mentioned as being involved in terrorist financing. But she couldn't say anything about that. 'All the more reason for you to hand yourself in now, clear your name, get it over with.'

They drank tea and repeated themselves for the next twenty minutes or so. Afterwards, as Daniel rinsed their mugs in the sink, he said, 'I'll think about it. There's something to be said for getting it over with. You're right about that. Also, the owners of this place will be back next week and I won't be able to go on camping here.'

'Will they expect all the work to be finished?'

'No but it's supposed to be farther forward than it is now. Maybe I'll think about handing myself in when I've caught up. Otherwise I'll be sitting in a police cell worrying about it.'

'I wouldn't wait if I were you,' said Sarah. 'Sooner the better.' They debated whether he should walk into a police station or simply return home. 'Where will you say you've been?'

'Staying with friends.'

'And when they ask which friends, where?'

'I won't say because I don't want to get them into trouble.'

'You could say you stayed in another mosque, which you won't identify for the same reason. You went there because you were frightened and didn't know what to do and wanted time to pray and contemplate and it was the imam who advised you to hand yourself in.'

Daniel smiled. 'Sounds as if you have some experience of this sort of thing. It could be true, too, if I'd thought of it.'

'Why not do it now, hand yourself in?'

He hesitated, then shrugged. 'Okay. If you give me a lift.'

They dropped him before the corner of his road, out of sight of his house and the police. His decision seemed not only to have cleared his mind but to have lightened it. He talked cheerfully on the way about building up his business, about going on the haj – the pilgrimage to Mecca that all Muslims were supposed to do once in their lifetimes – and about the difficulty of deciding when to start a family.

'That may be decided for you,' said Anya.

'If Allah wills.'

They left him hitching his tool-bag onto his shoulder and waving until they were out of sight.

'Well, that's a good job done,' said Anya. 'I can't thank you enough. Nor will Akela when she hears.'

'It took two of us. So long as he actually does it.'

'I think he will.'

Chapter Twelve

The restaurant was filling up. The rush would come at one o'clock when the Berlaymont and other EU offices emptied. It was like London in the 1970s and 1980s, when long liquid lunches were commonplace for middle and upper management and it would have been thought bizarre or sad to nibble a sandwich and salad at your desk while working. Charles had booked his table for 12.30, expecting Timber Wolf at 12.45. He had arrived ten minutes early to find a man and a woman in their thirties at the table nearest his and two men and a woman at the table nearest the door. Across the aisle from them sat a solitary older man reading *Le Monde*, a bottle of white wine opened and sampled before him. The place was blessedly free of background music but as more customers arrived the noise level rose enough to render eavesdropping difficult. Some of the tables had been moved since his last visit but separation was still just about adequate.

He had no idea whether the Z surveillance team was there when he arrived or whether they were among those still arriving and shaking their umbrellas on the doormat. Nor did he know how many of them there were. He didn't want to know anything about them, he had told Sonia when briefing her to set up the operation. He particularly didn't want to meet them and then recognise them again in Brussels. Not because he would have betrayed the fact – he was confident of that –but it could have been a distraction, as he knew from experience.

He had decided to call out a Z team over the weekend. They were a part-time resource, named after the Service's natural-cover Z Organisation of the 1930s, a parallel network unconnected to embassies and officialdom. It was staffed by people with real jobs in their real names, trained to undertake surveillance tasks in foreign jurisdictions where there was no local MI6 station or where its staff were too well-known to mount surveillance on their home territory. Or, as in this case, where the local station was kept in ignorance of the operation, along with the embassy and everyone else in Gareth Horley's former directorate. It would normally have been Gareth himself who authorised Z deployments and they would have been briefed by his staff, but Charles had bypassed normal structures for fear that Gareth might maintain unofficial contact with one or two of his colleagues who knew nothing of his current situation. In getting Sonia to do it on his behalf, Charles had insisted they be briefed and equipped not in any of the Service's London buildings but at the Castle, the south-coast training establishment.

'Hope you weren't planning a weekend,' he had said when ringing her at home.

Her sigh was audible. 'Feigned regret is worse than none, Charles. You've never been any good at it so don't start now.'

Timber Wolf arrived punctually, looming large in his Loden coat and tweed hat. He grinned and wiped his glasses on a red-and white-spotted handkerchief as he joined Charles at the table. 'You bring your English weather to Brussels. We are usually grateful for British imports but our negotiators should insist on a tariff on this one.'

'All part of the Brexit export drive. How long have you got?'

'Not long, less than an hour. We are very busy preparing for the next round of talks.'

They ordered straight away. Then, with a bottle of Timber Wolf's favourite Chianti open before them, Charles put his arms on the table and leaned forward. 'Thanks for fitting this in at such short notice, Eddie. I'm very grateful. I wouldn't have asked if it wasn't urgent.'

Timber Wolf nodded, his eyebrows slightly raised, his expression receptive. Charles took out his pocket diary, laying aside the folded piece of paper marking that day's page. He pretended to consult the short list he had written in the diary. 'There are three things. Firstly, Gareth. Have you heard from him?'

'No. Is he still ill?'

'No. At least, we don't think so, though it's possible. He was around at the end of last week and seemed okay but since then he's gone missing. We simply don't know where he is.'

Timber Wolf's small eyes widened behind his spectacles. He put down his glass and sat back. 'You mean he . . . you can't find him? He's not at home?'

'Not at home, not at work, not anywhere that we know of. And not a word to anyone. He hasn't tried to ring or email you or anything?'

'Not at all, I have heard nothing. Could it be an after-effect of his tropical illness that causes him to lose his memory or become depressed?'

'We don't know, we just don't know.'

'What was his illness, exactly?'

A good act, Charles thought, assuming it was one. Timber Wolf's question suggested confidence in his own abilities, perhaps over-confidence. Although a natural question, it was unnecessary, a self-indulgent tease designed to put Charles on the spot and see how he coped. 'Seems to have been one of those Third

World bugs in the bowel things, like liver-fluke but not liver-fluke. Not a fever, either, not something that turns the head, but debilitating, very debilitating. Has an exotic name I can't remember. Curable with drugs, fortunately, usually without after-effects but not invariably. We're at a loss for what to do.' He hoped his own act was as good. He wanted Timber Wolf to feel on top of things, to feel he was in control.

'Have you asked the police to help?'

'Yes. They've launched a missing persons inquiry and checked hospitals to see if he's had a heart attack or something, but no news.'

'How terrible for Suzanne.'

'She's worried sick, as you can imagine. You will let us know if you hear anything, won't you?'

'Of course, Charles, of course.'

They paused while the waiter served their penne carbonara and Charles pretended to consult his diary again. 'Next thing.' He leaned forward, lowering his voice. 'Your last report about the EU's bottom line aroused a great deal of interest and was much appreciated in the highest circles. I mean, the *highest circles*. I'm sure that doesn't surprise you?' Timber Wolf nodded and smiled. 'Now, I just want to make absolutely sure I got the figures right and I'd like you to go over again for me the circumstances in which you heard them. I'm sure you appreciate this is too important to permit of even the slightest error and that I need to assure the highest circles that everything I say is spot on.'

'Of course, I understand that.'

They went through what Timber Wolf had said before. He repeated himself, word for word. Another indication of rehearsed speech. Most people's true perceptions and recollections varied slightly in repeated tellings, especially under questioning. 'That's good, thank you,' Charles said. 'A great relief to me that I got it right. Imagine the consequences if I'd been a few billion out, either way.' They both laughed and drank. 'Consequences for the deal itself, of course, which would determine whether or not there's to be any deal at all. That's of central historical importance, that's the big one. But there would also be other consequences, less obvious but still important. Especially for Britain.' He drank again and pretended to concentrate on his food. He knew it had worked when, after a short while, Timber Wolf rested his knife and fork.

'What kind of other consequences?'

'All sorts of things.' Charles glanced at the table nearest them and leaned forward again, lowering his voice. 'Just to take one example – you won't repeat this to anyone, will you? Promise me you'll guard your lips.'

Timber Wolf smiled and put his large hands over his ears. 'I'll guard my ears, too, if you like, so I don't even hear it.'

Charles spoke slowly and with pauses, as if struggling to recall correctly. It must not sound rehearsed. 'Knowing the EU fallback position means that a major rift in the cabinet in London has now been healed. Since there's no question of paying that much – they're all united on that – the chancellor has opened his wallet and agreed to spend billions that would have gone into the divorce settlement on preparing for a hard Brexit, divorce without a deal. Previously, he wouldn't agree to spend anything serious on it apart from the few million already announced because neither he nor half the cabinet believed it was going to happen. Didn't want it to, anyway. Still don't. But your report convinced them that a deal is now impossible on the terms the EU insists on. They'd never get it through Parliament or the country and it would split the party. It hasn't been announced and won't be but the truth is they've given up on getting a deal.'

'You mean they're calling off the talks, walking away?'

'No, no, they'll keep talking to the last second of the last minute of the last hour. They're determined to show willing. But they now believe that a deal is impossible.'

Timber Wolf's moon face creased in concern. It was as if Charles had confessed to a fatal illness. He had picked up his knife and fork again but hesitated to eat. 'They didn't – they don't have a figure in mind, something they would accept?'

Charles shrugged. 'Can't say. For one thing, I'm not party to cabinet discussions and for another, even if I were, my lips would be sealed.'

'But do you think they might have a figure in mind? They must have some idea of what would be acceptable in order to know that the EU figure isn't. You haven't heard anyone saying anything, any speculation?'

'None that I know to be reliable. People talk, obviously, but ...' He shrugged again and drank more wine, aware that Timber Wolf still held his knife and fork in suspension and was watching him closely. The role reversal was going as he had hoped, with Timber Wolf, in his eagerness to have something significant to report back, becoming the debriefing case officer and Charles the agent. His longing for the big bone to take back to his masters had blunted Timber Wolf's awareness.

'What do people say?' he asked.

'Oh, all sorts of things. Gossip inflated by self-importance and coloured by wishful thinking. You must be familiar with that sort of stuff. But it's why you're so good, Eddie. You see through it all, you only report what you actually know.' He stood. 'Must just go to the loo. Excuse me a moment.'

Timber Wolf nodded and went back to work with his knife and fork. Charles left the table, then turned back after a couple of paces to retrieve his diary. 'Age,' he said with a smile. 'Doing it more and more. I know it would be safe with you but I mustn't let myself make a habit of it.' He picked up his diary, leaving the folded paper he had used to mark the page between his plate and side-plate, partly obscured by each. He didn't hurry in the loo.

'Third thing,' he said as he took his seat back at the table, 'also concerns Gareth. It's a rather sensitive subject that I wouldn't normally mention but for the fact that you've known him a long time. There have been certain stories, allegations – call them what you will – in London about his behaviour with women in the office. Nothing sensational, no rape claims or assaults or anything like that, nothing involving the police. Not so far, anyway. It's more allegations of persistent unwanted attention amounting to harassment. That seems to be the vogue word for it, though I'm not personally convinced it amounts to that. But then I'm rather old-fashioned when it comes to such matters, as I'm constantly reminded. The reason I'm telling you this is that if – when – he does turn up he'll probably have to face some sort of inquiry by the staff counsellor, a Cabinet Office official who handles staff complaints from within the intelligence agencies. I shall do my best to protect him, of course – especially given whatever's going on in his head now – but I need to know how much truth there is in these allegations. They could be exaggerated, they could be under-estimates, I just don't know. What would help is if you could tell me whether you've ever noticed such tendencies in your long acquaintance.'

Timber Wolf resumed his concerned expression. 'No, I have never noticed this. He likes women, of course – he is not alone – but he has always behaved very well with them when I have been with him and I am sure he is devoted to Suzanne.'

'No indications that he has ever been unfaithful?'

'None at all, no. I can't imagine it.'

'Thanks, Eddie, that's very helpful. It will help me argue his case in his absence.' He raised his glass. 'Here's to Gareth, in the hope that he turns up safe and well and doesn't come back to some godawful mess and scandal.'

Timber Wolf looked serious. 'To Gareth, our good friend. Now I must go, Charles.'

'You must. Thank you for coming. I am much reassured.' He put his elbows on the table, palms upwards. 'But there is something I must apologise for. Your expenses. I was in such a rush that I forgot to put them in an envelope. Do you mind if we shake hands across the table? I don't think anyone will notice.'

Timber Wolf smiled as they shook hands and the notes were transferred from palm to palm, not quite invisibly. 'It is like an old spy film.'

'Very like.' Charles smiled. 'Next time I'll remember the envelope, I promise.' He took out his diary. 'Now, when should that be? Soon, I hope.' They agreed a date and Timber Wolf left. Charles called for the bill and a coffee, picked up the folded sheet of paper, still half concealed beneath his plates, and glanced again at the figures and cryptic notes, written as in haste:

EU secret bottom line = sum we offered + 80%.
Our secret upper limit = SWO + 20%.
Poss compromise – would we accept SWO + 50%
    if EU come down?
Vote – yes 8, no 0.
PM – if they won't do we walk away or pay
    SWO + 80%?
For. Sec. – walk away. Home Sec. – accept.
    Chancellor – accept.
Vote – WA 4, accepts 4.
PM casting vote – WA.

He carefully re-folded the note and put it back in his diary.

Thirty minutes later he was back in his hotel. It was still raining and there were few tourists among the umbrellas hurrying back from lunch. He imagined Timber Wolf in his meeting, anxious for it to end so that he could report his lunchtime's work. There was a soft knock at his door. He let Sonia in. 'You're wet,' he said when the door was closed.

'What a good spy you'd make. So observant.' She stood her dripping umbrella in the bath and took off her coat. 'Tea, since you offered. I'm dying for the loo. D'you mind?' She closed the door.

Afterwards she sat in an armchair, he at the narrow desk. He waited for her to start. 'Don't say you have nothing to tell me.'

'Question is, where to begin.' She sipped her tea. 'Well, he seems to have swallowed your bait, hook, line and sinker. As soon as you were safely out of sight in the loo he reached over, unfolded your piece of paper, read it, took out his phone, looked round to see if anyone was watching, then photographed it and put it carefully back just as you'd left it. He actually looked straight at the team who were filming him. Obviously didn't realise.'

'They got him in the act? Where were they sitting?'

'I don't know exactly because I wasn't there, of course. They say they weren't the nearest table to you but were diagonally across and farther in, away from the door, facing him rather than you. They got you paying him, too. The banknotes were just visible.'

'And then they followed him back to his office? The team outside, I mean.'

'No.'

'No?'

'He didn't go to his office. He went to a block of flats in the suburbs. The block where it just so happens that Christine, Gareth's mistress, lives. They couldn't confirm he actually went to her flat – we know which it is, thanks to Cheltenham – but he took the lift to the same floor.'

'Thank them from me. Thank them.' Charles put down his cup. 'So maybe Gareth's holing up there and Timber Wolf was telling him before reporting to his own masters. Interesting priority.'

'Letting him know what you said about him, most likely. Threat of arrest or harassment investigations and all that. So he's not going to be tempted to sneak back to the UK in a hurry. He was only there about twenty minutes – Timber Wolf – then he returned to his office.'

Charles stood and walked over to the window, hands in pockets. 'So the trap is sprung. The other side have secretly discovered our secret top line through what they think is their own operation and are convinced – we hope – that we'll leave without a deal rather than go above it. Both of which happen to be true. It's what we want them to believe and we want them to know we mean it. Espionage is once again the midwife of truth. Very gratifying, don't you think?'

'But what next? What do we do about Gareth?'

'Nothing. Leave him to stew in his own juice. No need for me to see him now.'

'And let him spill the beans about all our Brexit thinking?'

'Of course. So long as they've swallowed the big one, the rest doesn't matter. Most of it will become apparent in horse-trading across the negotiating table, anyway.

In fact, it's better he stays here than comes back. If he returns it's trouble for us and trouble for him.'

'And for Suzanne?'

'Tough on Suzanne but that's his problem. He created it. Nothing we can do about it. We can't save his marriage for him.'

'But it's not just Brexit he could spill the beans on. It's all our other ops, worldwide.'

'He wouldn't do that.'

'Wouldn't he? What's to stop him? He might not have begun with that intention but minds may be changed by circumstance.'

He had known this all along, of course, but had pushed it to the back of his own mind because, despite all that Gareth had done to surprise and disappoint him, he could not believe that that would ever have been his intention. But she was right: intentions, reasons, motives, excuses, justifications were often the pawns of circumstance. Consistency in human affairs should never be taken for granted. Anyone was capable of anything, he remembered saying, though he wasn't quite sure whether he believed it. The other reason he had not thought about what Gareth might do was that the consequences were too awful to contemplate.

Sonia got up and stood by the window with him, arms folded. 'You know who I mean by Tessa Mountfield?'

'No. Unless you mean the journalist? I don't know

her.' She was a freelance journalist well known for a series of television interviews with corporate whistle-blowers who claimed, with varying justification, to have been victims of malfeasance, impropriety or injustice.

'That's the lady. She's here, in Brussels, seen at the block of flats that Gareth's mistress lives in. The team recognised her getting out of a taxi as they were following Timber Wolf away from the building.'

'Doesn't mean she's going to see Gareth.'

'Except that we now know her mobile is on his private mobile's contact list.'

'Since when?'

'Since before he disappeared.'

'He never said anything about knowing her.' Staff were supposed to declare contact with journalists. 'Could be coincidence. Coincidences do happen.'

'Save that one for the inquiry.'

'If we intervene now – if I go and see him – it risks blowing what we're doing, the whole thing.'

'And if he's spilling the beans to her and we don't?'

Chapter Thirteen

Charles paused outside the door of flat 26, listening for voices. The black paintwork was smart, the silvered bell-button polished. He had escaped challenge by the concierge downstairs by taking advantage of an altercation with a delivery driver who the concierge insisted should move his van from outside the front door. Hearing nothing within, he pressed the bell.

There was no response, no footsteps, no opening or closing of doors. He waited and pressed again. This time he heard a loo flush, then a door close, then steps, then silence. There was a flicker of movement behind the peephole, then more steps. Finally, the door was opened by Gareth Horley.

'Come in, Charles.' He smiled. He looked relaxed and youthful in jeans, trainers and a blue Guernsey, much as when they had run cases together. He was ageing well, physically. The difference was that this time he was pointing a pistol at Charles's stomach. 'I've been half-expecting you.'

Charles didn't move. 'What's that for?'

'Just a precaution, sensible in my new circumstances. Don't worry, I'm not about to do anything silly.' He stepped back, holding the door open and lowering the pistol.

Charles entered and, at a nod from Gareth, headed left along the parquet-floored hall into a large light sitting room. The single wide window looked across the road to the canal and fields beyond. There were no boats or barges on the canal. A herd of Friesians grazed in the field. Charles turned to face Gareth, his hands in the pockets of his British Warm overcoat. He nodded at the pistol. 'Does Christine know about this?'

Gareth shook his head. 'Need to know. Smuggled it back with me from the Balkans. D'you remember I was out there? Exciting times. No end of kit like this knocking around, pistols two a penny. Bigger stuff, too.'

'Why?'

Gareth shrugged. 'Well, it was available, it was easy, kind of a memento, really. And I thought, well, you never know, might come in handy one day.'

'Christine wouldn't be very happy, would she? Make quite a mess in a nice apartment like this.' It was a feminine room in mainly pastel colours with a sofa, two armchairs and a polished round dining table and chairs. Two seventeenth-century Dutch interiors hung on adjacent walls in elaborate gilt frames.

'That's true, she doesn't like mess. But there should be no need for it, I hope. Take off your coat and sit down.'

It was more an order than an invitation. Charles took off his coat, folded it over the back of the sofa and went to sit in one of the dining chairs. He could get up more quickly from one of those.

Gareth gestured casually with the pistol. 'You'll find an armchair or the sofa more comfortable.' He sat in a dining chair, side on to the table, facing Charles.

Charles chose the sofa, leaning back against his coat and trying not to appear mesmerised by the pistol. He wanted to appear to concentrate on Gareth's face as if disregarding the pistol, but in fact he never let it out of his vision. It was squat and black, a semi-automatic, not a model he recognised, probably Russian or Eastern European. 'I'd forgotten you were in the Balkans. You were head of station, weren't you?'

'My first station. Worked closely with the army. Really enjoyed it. Heady times. Where were you then?'

'Nairobi, probably. Maybe South Africa. No, that was earlier.' They were eight or nine feet apart, too far for him to leap up and make a grab for the gun. Gareth knew what he was doing. They would have done the same rudimentary self-defence training when they joined, basic stuff but enough to instil a few simple lessons such as that the point of a gun was to kill at a distance and if you let anyone close enough to grab it you had lost the advantage it gave you.

Gareth sat with his legs crossed, his left elbow on the table, the gun in his right hand and resting in his lap. He seemed at ease with it, with himself and with Charles. 'Timber Wolf enjoyed the lunch you gave him. Very happy bunny. Showed me what he'd got.'

Charles had already decided to feign ignorance. 'What had he got?'

'The notes, the figures and thinking on the paper you so carelessly left for him to find. Not like the old Charles I knew. Becoming chief must have blunted your operational edge. Nice touch, though. He's like a dog with two tails. Couldn't wait to report back.'

There was no point in further pretence. Gareth would treat denial with contempt. 'What did you say to him about it?'

'Don't worry, I didn't give your little game away. Not yet, anyway. If that's what London wants them to think, that's fine by me. No skin off my nose. Probably even has the virtue of being true, doesn't it?'

'And will Tessa Mountfield be equally pleased? I understand she's been here.'

Gareth paused, then recovered with a smile. 'Put surveillance on me, have you? Really pulling out all the stops. Local station or a Z team? The latter, I hope. Safer. They need the exercise, anyway.'

'What are you doing with her?'

'Reinsurance. In case I can't return to London without suffering the indignity of inquiries and inquisitions. We had an introductory talk, that's all. She knows in general what I've got for sale but no detail, as yet. If she and the outfits she works for buy my story I should be able to survive – maybe even thrive – abroad in reasonable comfort.'

'Which story? You must have many to choose from.'

'All of them. Everything. My career. All the operations I know about or have been involved with, past and present. Not just the one that brings you here, which would be big enough on its own. There's plenty of others, Operation Tresco, for instance. How's that submission going, by the way? Are they going to let our old friend Herm do his job?' When Charles didn't respond he smiled again. 'Fancy a drink?'

Charles shook his head. Gareth poured from a half-full bottle of whisky on the table that Charles hadn't noticed before. There were several glasses by it. What Gareth was now contemplating was a clear breach of the Official Secrets Act, which would mean prison if he set foot in the UK again. Outside UK jurisdiction, even within the EU, it might be difficult to enforce, and if he chose to flee to Russia, impossible. 'Why, Gareth?'

'Why what?'

'Why all this? I don't get it. Why have you gone off the rails, fiddled Timber Wolf's payments for money

231

you don't need, exaggerated your reporting when the bare bones would have been sufficient, got yourself into trouble with girls in the Office, set up here with Christine when you could have her without turning your life upside down, taken to that' – Charles nodded at the whisky – 'and let yourself be used by Timber Wolf and the EU? You must have sensed what they were up to, suspected it anyway, but you never said anything. It wouldn't have counted against you if you had – you'd have got credit for it, Brownie points, more than. You were well thought of in the Office and in Whitehall, in line for my job; I was going to recommend you. Your marriage was okay and you had a mistress here whom no one suspected. And now what you're contemplating is going to put you in prison. Either that or the misery of endless self-justification in Moscow or somewhere, despised by everyone whose good opinion you previously sought. It's not as if you're a fanatical Remainer, seeing the EU as the only right and practical cause and British disaffection as self-defeating xenophobia. It's not that, is it, Gareth? You don't even have a cause.'

'I was – am – a Remainer.'

'So are lots of people, in the Office, in Whitehall, everywhere, about forty-eight per cent of them. But they don't do this. You could have resigned and campaigned for it if you felt that strongly. But you don't, do you, not really? So, why? Tell me. If you can.'

Charles's tone was deliberately taunting. When confronted by a madman with a gun best keep talking. It seemed to be working. The bottle clinked against the rim of his glass as Gareth poured himself more whisky with his left hand. His right still rested in his lap, holding the pistol on its side, pointing along the top of his thigh at Charles. 'Hard to say,' he said. 'Self-analysis has never really been my thing. Nor yours, I suspect. Self-indulgent waste of time. We're trapped within ourselves. Analysis can't be trusted when that which is to be analysed is what purports to be doing the analysing. You can't step outside yourself. I am what I am. Why do you think I'm doing it? You have a go.'

'I can't say. You can't follow someone into madness, which is where you seem to be heading.' He had been wrong about Daniel, he now realised. Daniel was not mad, just a bit nutty. This was something else. 'I had thought – I thought you were someone else.'

'So I was but I'm also this. Always was, I guess, but didn't always do anything about it. Both sides of me exist, both are true. Anyone can be anything. Haven't I heard you say that?'

'Probably.'

'But I suppose a psychiatrist would say it goes back a long way with me. That's their usual creed, isn't it? In my case, back to the Welsh valleys of my parents, the council estate I was brought up in, then a choral scholarship to the choir school, then my voice broke and

I was sent to the local comprehensive. Imagine that, if you can. Choir school to comp. That was tough. I learned I had to fight for everything in daily life and fight even harder if I wanted to get on. Then getting to university, then getting into the Office, the heart of the establishment, peopled by privileged public schoolboys like you—'

'Grammar. I come from Buckinghamshire.'

'Same difference if you come from where I come from. Getting on is something you can take for granted but for me it was what it meant to be alive. The struggle was life, life was struggle. And having got on, you fight to get farther on. There's no end until you end. You have no idea how much I want – wanted – to be chief, and how much I resented you for getting it. Especially as you'd already left. Fluke, wasn't it? Complete fluke, you must admit.'

Charles nodded.

'It would have been the same if I'd got it. I couldn't stop fighting, you see, struggling to get ahead even when I was already there.'

It was all a bit too pat, too self-exculpatory, as if Gareth had long been persuading himself. 'But fiddling Timber Wolf's salary and expenses? Pinching and keeping an illegal weapon? That's not getting ahead, that's petty crime. Haven't been done for shop-lifting, have you? Not to mention touching up girls in the Office.'

Gareth put his glass down sharply on the table. 'I never touched up anyone who didn't want to be touched.'

'That's not what they're saying in London.' It fell into the category of necessary lies, Charles decided. 'Anyway, none of that is the Gareth Horley I knew, thought I knew. The Gareth who ran the Herm, Likely Lad and Red Beret cases. Things we did together.' He indicated the whisky. 'Is that what's happened to you, Gareth? Is that what's at the bottom of it?'

'Despite appearances, no, it isn't. Not fundamentally. Christine happened to me, that's what happened.'

'But she's been happening for quite a long time, hasn't she? Since Geneva?'

'You've done your homework. Full marks. Grammar-school swot.'

'You haven't done yours, Gareth. Whatever your motives, whatever you're planning, it can't work. You'll spend the rest of your life a fugitive, getting poorer. You'll lose your self-respect. Losing the respect of others is bad enough but loss of self-respect is fatal, you never get it back.' Keep talking, he was thinking all the time. Waffle on, no matter what the waffle. Talk postponed action. Gareth would probably act only when he had convinced himself there was no alternative, so keep providing one. 'But I still don't understand why, Gareth. What really prompted you. Background isn't enough. It's all too pat. Millions of people were brought up on council estates and went to local comps and are successful and honest. As were you, once. What changed?'

'I'm not sure I was, you see, not ever, not inside, anyway. Like I was saying just now. I never actually did anything before but I was always aware of the potential within, always knew I would somehow, always felt I was different. Outwardly I was one of you, but inwardly I was not.'

'But aren't we all like that? We're all inners and outers, all different. You're one of us after all, Gareth, you're not different.' Gareth seemed attentive, engaged. Perhaps it was working. 'Look, why don't you just put the gun away and let's discuss sensibly how we're going to proceed, what the best future for you is. Chuck the gun in the canal. It's never going to do you any good.'

Gareth looked down at the gun in his lap, as if noticing it for the first time. When he looked up he was smiling. 'Right now what I'm considering, Charles, is whether to shoot myself or you.'

Charles compressed his lips and shrugged in feigned indifference. 'What's the point in either?'

'You're logical, I'll say that for you. Always have been. Perhaps I should do us both? Or toss for it.'

'How much have you drunk today?'

'No more than usual.' He let go of his whisky, transferred the gun to his left hand, keeping it pointed at Charles, reached into his trouser pocket with his right and fished out a coin. 'Let's toss, shall we?' He proffered it to Charles, holding it between thumb and forefinger.

Charles yawned. Yawning was often a nervous reaction with him. In the army he had yawned repeatedly while sitting, cramped, in the roaring turbulence of a C-130 Hercules, waiting to jump out. He shook his head.

'Suit yourself.' Gareth flicked the coin into the air. 'Heads it's me, tails it's you.' It landed on the thick pile carpet midway between them. 'What is it?'

'I can't see from here.' If he could get Gareth to leave his chair and bend down he might –might – be able to jump him.

'You look.'

Charles didn't move. He imagined getting off the sofa, bending to pick up the coin and being shot in the top of his head.

Gareth transferred the gun back to his right hand and extended his arm, pointing it steadily at Charles. 'Go on, do as I say. No surprises, I promise.'

For a few seconds Charles still didn't move. He was calculating whether, if he got up to get the coin, he would be close enough to make a grab for the gun. Not quite, he reckoned. On the other hand, better chance that than stay where he was and be shot on the sofa. After all, it was possible that it was all bluff, that the gun wasn't loaded. Though he doubted that.

He got up slowly, took two paces forward and stooped to pick up the coin. It was a pound; he had assumed it would be a euro. He could see as he bent down that it was tails. He turned it as he picked it up. 'Heads,' he said, holding it out slightly to his left so that Gareth would have to turn his head to see. That would be his chance.

But Gareth did not turn his head. Instead, he sighed, raised his eyebrows and settled farther back in his chair, relaxing. 'Always trusted you to tell the truth, Charles. Always have.' He put the pistol to his right temple, midway between ear and eye, and fired.

The noise was concussing, a physical shock that seemed to shake the room. Gareth's head jerked sideways and blood and other matter splattered across the table, some of it reaching the wall. There was the instant familiar smell of a discharged firearm, mixed with something sweeter. Charles stood with his left arm still outstretched and holding the coin with the Queen's head turned upwards. Gareth's body slumped in the chair, lolling sideways, his head coming to rest against the back of it, his left elbow still on the table, his right arm hanging limp. The gun fell to the carpet with a muffled thump.

Charles could not say afterwards how long he had stood looking at the body. It might have been only seconds, certainly less than a minute. He remembered a couple of inconsequential thoughts that offered themselves while he was thinking there was no point in attempting resuscitation. One was that Gareth had shot himself as Hitler had, with a pistol to the right temple, and that perhaps Hitler had looked as Gareth looked now, slumped and lifeless. The other was that he should pocket the coin rather than return it to Gareth's trousers with his fingerprints on it. That, on reflection, was not so inconsequential after all. He pocketed the coin and tiptoed out into the hall, as if it were necessary not to wake Gareth.

He paused by the telephone, which rested on a small table near the front door. The concierge had not seen him enter the block; he ought to be able to find a way of leaving unseen. He had not left fingerprints on anything except perhaps the doorbell, which could be wiped. The last people to have seen Gareth alive would be Timber Wolf and Tessa Mountfield, who would no doubt be able to give good accounts of themselves. It wasn't as if the Office owed Timber Wolf any loyalty, anyway.

Only Sonia knew Charles was there. He could safely tell her what had happened and then decide whether to report in full when he returned to London, with all the legal ramifications that might ensue, or whether to omit any mention of having seen Gareth and await announcements in the Belgian press of the suicide of a visiting British diplomat.

Or he could do what was right and proper: ring the

Belgian police and tell them exactly what had happened, minus the spying. Gareth would be presented as a senior official known to have a drink problem and suspected of undergoing some sort of breakdown, the balance of his mind presumably disturbed. Charles, as colleague and old friend, had followed him to Brussels to try to persuade him to seek treatment. During their conversation Gareth had got drunk and then abruptly shot himself, his last words being something like, 'I've had enough of everything.' There would be a deal of administrative to-ing and fro-ing but nothing seriously problematic. It would probably reach the press that the chief of MI6 was the key witness and conspiracy theorists – perhaps including a disappointed Tessa Mountfield – would make much of it. He could live with that.

On the other hand, when Timber Wolf and his masters realised that Charles knew where Gareth was hiding and was in touch with him they might suspect they were being sold a pup, and so mistrust the secrets they had been so pleased to have discovered. That, in turn, might jeopardise the chances of a Brexit deal.

Charles hesitated by the phone.

Chapter Fourteen

'Seems to have worked, or be working,' said the foreign secretary, pulling at his earlobe as he glanced at a paper on the desk before him. 'So far, anyway. Latest from the negotiations is that both sides are inching towards agreement like a pair of suspicious sloths.'

They were not in the Foreign Office but in the foreign secretary's smaller, panelled office in Parliament, one of several in corridors behind the speaker's chair. There was no private secretary, just him, Robin Woodstock and Charles. 'You did the right thing in Brussels,' he continued, glancing up at Charles. 'Don't you think, Robin?'

'Not sure about right in the larger sense,' said Robin. 'That's beyond my pay grade. But what he did worked, so it's right in that sense.'

'And the lawyers are happy?'

'The lawyers say they have nothing to say about it. For once.'

'Because they're afraid to commit themselves?'

'Probably.' Robin shrugged and turned to Charles. 'This is not in any way to detract from your sterling contribution to the national weal but I'm pretty sure the sort of agreement that's emerging would have emerged anyway, one way or another. More slowly, perhaps, and with more scope for things to go wrong, but something very like it.'

''Course it would,' said the foreign secretary, 'because what we were selling them was the truth. We just gave them a helping hand to realise it. It's just as Charles said – successful spying makes everyone happy. They mounted an operation against us to persuade us of their bottom line, we turned it against them and used it to persuade them of our top line and of our preparedness to walk away without a deal and without paying a single centime – which, though true, was what neither of us wanted – and so both sides decided to settle for the halfway house that was always the sensible solution. We may not be there yet but we shall be so long as – as Charles also said – none of this comes out. It's only when spying is discovered that people are unhappy. That's right, isn't it?'

Charles nodded. He wasn't sure he had said anything in quite those terms but was happy that the foreign secretary, a magpie with other people's ideas and phrases, should make his case for him.

'Talking of which, you know that Tresco submission

got the green light?' the foreign secretary continued. 'The prime minister agreed that that murdering bastard should be bumped off with help from your man Herm. He flayed a man, you know, flayed him alive, the murdering bastard.'

'I had heard, yes. Before I went to Brussels.'

'Well, it's happened. He was zapped by an RAF drone. We heard this morning from the MOD, hasn't been announced yet. Your Herm chap managed the phone switch-over and the new phone beckoned the drone in and it got him. The flayer, that is. Hope Herm got himself out of the way in time.'

'So do I. We should have heard by now. I'll find out whether he's been in contact when I get back to the office.'

'There was another chap zapped as well, another Brit. In the same car, apparently. No name yet but it turns out this chap was delivering the new phones from this so-called charity that's been supplying the so-called Islamic State with kit intended for real charities. Police and Charity Commission have been investigating it for some time. Going to be closed down now.'

'Definitely another Brit?'

The foreign secretary nodded and glanced at his phone as it buzzed. 'Division coming up. We are bidden to vote.' He stood. 'Only other thing is your future, Charles. Now that Mr Horley has removed himself from the succession we need to find someone else. Attempts have been made—'

'Informal soundings only,' said Robin. 'No one has yet been invited to apply.'

'. . . but it appears there's not exactly a stampede. No one wants the job, no one suitable, anyway. Bit too early for your new director of operations, your Sonia Something lady, to be in the frame for it, I suppose? Apparently this stuff the Russians have been putting out about MI6 knocking off its own number two because he wanted out has been putting applicants off. Not helped by those articles by that Tessa Mountain woman. Amazing what nonsense people will believe. Lucky no one's put you in the frame for it. Lucky for the negotiations, too.' The division rang loudly. The foreign secretary moved towards the door, tucking his shirt tail into his trousers. 'Thanks for your good work, Charles. Looks like you may have to stay on. For a while, anyway.'

'He means it, I'm afraid,' said Robin as the door closed. 'The cabinet secretary would like you to stay. But up to you, of course. And Sarah. She presumably has a dog in the fight?'

It was months later when Charles and Sarah attended another function at Anya's parents' Wimbledon house. It was a more subdued affair than the wedding, though with many of the same people. Neither funeral nor wake, it was billed as a celebration of Daniel's life and for Akela and the child she was expecting. The weather was no longer warm enough for it to be held on the lawn, but the house was large and the French windows were open onto the terrace.

Anya's parents were generous, making every effort not only for their widowed daughter but for Daniel's family and friends. Anya's father spoke fulsomely and sensitively, followed by Daniel's estranged father, who spoke briefly and adequately. Deborah stood beside him, immaculate as ever but silent, her face thinner and more lined.

'She's coping very well,' said Sarah afterwards as they drove back to Westminster. 'I really admire her for it. Bad enough losing him but no funeral means no closure. It was so kind of Anya's and Akela's parents to do this. Was it really impossible to recover anything of the body?'

Charles had seen photographs taken from the drone that fired the missile. All the occupants of the car – there were two others unknown – had been instantaneously dissolved into the atoms from which they were constituted. The car itself was barely recognisable as such. 'There would have been nothing left. Anyway, it was in IS territory so no one could have collected it if there had been anything.'

'Have they ever worked out how Daniel got out of the country?'

'Not really. Last I heard from MI5 they thought it

might have been via Ireland. They think he left London the day you and Anya saw him. Must have had places to hide on the way.'

'They don't still think he was really doing it, knowingly supplying terrorists, do they?'

'MI5 don't, as I said before. The police are more reluctant to declare him innocent.'

'I told Deborah you'd said MI5 think he was an innocent victim manipulated by the people in that mosque. So far as he was concerned he was doing real charity work. That might be some comfort to her, if anything can be.' She paused. 'But he might have realised when he got there, don't you think? They can't have seemed like ordinary charity people.'

Nor did they, according to Herm, who had found plausible reason to distance himself after secretly substituting Tresco/1's phone. He had seen Daniel but not spoken to him, describing him as quiet and subdued, probably intimidated, speaking no Arabic. Herm had the impression that Daniel knew something was wrong – perhaps knew by then that everything was wrong – but had no idea how to get out of it. He was virtually a prisoner. Herm had heard Tresco/1 and the other two discussing what to do with him, whether he was worth a ransom to anyone, or whether they could put him to work, or to death. Tresco/1 just said, 'Come with us, brother,' in English, when they were getting in the car. They were the only words anyone said to him in Herm's presence. The drone must have already logged on to the phone's signal and the controller was presumably waiting until the car was well away from any buildings or other vehicles in order to minimise collateral damage.

Later, as they drove along the Embankment, Sarah said, 'I'm never sure about the morality of these drone things. I know you say it's ethically no different from a fighter pilot spotting an enemy vehicle and bombing it but it's so cold-blooded, just a controller sitting in a booth thousands of miles away, safe and sound, not risking himself at all. It's waging war without fighting. Doesn't seem fair.'

'They kill fewer innocents than bombs or bullets or shells, more precise, more accurate. But I agree, I wouldn't like to have to do it.'

'You – you, the Office, I mean – don't get involved in this sort of operation, do you? The sort that killed Daniel.'

Charles paused as he turned into Smith Square, pulling round a taxi that was disgorging evening concertgoers. He had never lied to Sarah. He didn't now, not literally, except by omission. He wasn't sure whether that counted. 'Drones are MOD operations. They actually do them. Them or the Americans.'

So much for midwifery, he thought as he parked. You couldn't always choose what you delivered.

ABOUT THE AUTHOR

Alan Judd is a novelist and biographer who has previously served in the army and at the Foreign Office. Chosen as one of the original twenty Best Young British Novelists, he subsequently won the Royal Society of Literature's Winifred Holtby Award, the Heinemann Award and the *Guardian* Fiction Award; he was also shortlisted for the Westminster Prize. Two of his novels, *Breed of Heroes* and *Legacy*, were filmed for the BBC and a third, *The Kaiser's Last Kiss*, has been filmed as *The Exception*, starring Christopher Plummer and Lily James. Alan Judd has reviewed widely, was a comment writer for the *Daily Telegraph* and writes the motoring column for *The Oldie*.

**Don't miss Alan Judd's brilliantly
plotted, pulse-racing novel featuring
Charles Thoroughgood**

DEEP BLUE

During a time of political disruption and rising
anti-nuclear sentiment, MI5 discovers that an
extremist fringe group, Action Against Austerity,
appears to have links to an established political party
while planning sabotage using something or someone
called Deep Blue. Banned from investigating British
political parties, the head of MI5 seeks advice from
Charles Thoroughgood, his opposite number in MI6.

Agreeing to help unofficially with the case,
Charles must delve deep into his own past,
to an unresolved Cold War case linked to his
private life. Using the past as key to the present,
he soon finds himself in a race against time to
prevent a plot which is politically nuclear . . .

SIMON &
SCHUSTER

Chapter One

The Present

Agent files – paper files, anyway – told stories. It was never quite the whole story – nothing was ever that – and they could be misleading, repetitive and elliptical, but as you opened the buff covers and fingered the flimsy pages of carbon-copied letters and contact notes, and the thicker pages of Head Office minutes or telegrams from MI6 stations, a skeleton became a body and eventually a person. It was the story of a relationship; sometimes, almost, of a life. And sometimes, as with the file that Charles Thoroughgood sat hunched over that evening, it bore the ghostly impress of another story, an expurgated presence that had shaped the present one without ever being mentioned.

Files rarely lied in terms of content; their lies were usually by omission, nearly always on security grounds.

In this case Charles knew those grounds well, having written much of what was in the file, and nearly all of what wasn't, many years before.

Pellets of rain splattered against his office window, invisible behind the blinds he had insisted upon despite assurances that the security glass could not be seen through. Having spent much of his operational career penetrating the allegedly impenetrable, he was reluctant to accept blanket security assurances. The more confident the assertion, the less he trusted it, and now, as Chief of MI6, he was better able to assert his prejudices than at any point in his eccentric and unpredictable ascent to the top. But not as much as he would have liked; Head Office was still in Croydon and the government seemed in no hurry to fulfil its promise of a return to Whitehall.

He was on volume three of the file, the final volume, reading more slowly as he neared the point where he had joined the case as a young officer on the Paris station during the Cold War. He was alone in the Office but for the guards and a few late-stayers, having sent his private secretary home. Sarah, his wife, was also working late, the common fate of City lawyers. The file was a relief from his screen with its unending emails and spreadsheets; also an escape into a world which, because it was past, seemed now so much simpler and clearer than the present. But it had seemed neither simple nor clear then.

There was no hint of a link to another file, no reference to papers removed. When at last he found what he sought he moved the green-shaded desk lamp closer and sat back in his chair, the file on his lap. Movement reactivated the overhead lights, which he disliked for their harshness, but if he stayed still for long enough they would go out. The desk lamp he had brought in himself, against the rules.

The paper he sought was in two sections, the first typed in Russian in Cyrillic script, the second a translation into English by someone from the Russian desk in Century House, the old Head Office during much of the Cold War. They should not have been in this file at all, an ordinary numbered P file belonging to a dead access agent run by the Paris station. Josef, as Charles had known him, was a Russian émigré who, unusually, had been allowed out of the Soviet Union on marrying a secretary from the French Embassy. Before that he was a journalist who had committed some minor indiscretion which had earned him ten years in a labour camp, in the days when ten years was what you got for being available to fill a quota, especially if you were Jewish. Settled in France, he had come to the notice of the Paris station, which had recruited him to get alongside visiting Russians. The relationship with the Secret Intelligence Service lasted many years, sustained by snippets from Josef which usually promised more than they delivered, and by payments from SIS, before Charles was sent to terminate him. That was when the case became interesting.

The paper did not, in fact, pertain to Josef at all, though that would not have been apparent to anyone reading the file. It was recorded that Josef had been in a labour camp, so a first-person account of a visit to the camp years after it had closed would be assumed to be his. The account had been left on Josef's file after other papers had been silently removed, doubtless because whoever weeded the file had made the same mistaken assumption. By the time Charles had discovered it, both Josef and Badger, code-name of the author of the paper, were dead. It might have drawn attention to the Badger case to have transferred papers to it years later. Not that anyone read old paper files any more. Charles was probably the only person still serving who knew both cases.

There was no real need for him to re-read Badger's account of his visit to his former prison camp. Charles remembered it well enough and his renewed interest in the case now, so many years later, was not because of that. He read it partly because he was nostalgic, partly to revive his sense of the man known as Badger, whose own file he had yet to re-read, and partly in penance, acknowledgement of unfulfilled promise. The description of the camp visit was intended by Badger to be part of the memoir he never wrote, an indication of what he hoped to publish when safely resettled in the

West. But he never was resettled and this was the only chapter written. Charles had promised that, if anything happened to Badger, he would see it published somewhere. And never had.

Turning to the typewritten English translation, marked by Tippexed alterations and the translator's margin comments in pencil, Charles read:

Since I was in that remote region, the region of my last camp, and with time to spare before the flight back to Moscow, I told my driver to take me to it. He was puzzled. 'There's nothing there, it was closed years ago. Just the huts and the wire and some of the old guards who have nowhere else to go.'

'Take me.'

It was farther from the airport than I thought and there was fresh snow, unmarked by other car tracks. It was fortunate that the driver knew the way because I should never have found it, hidden in a clearing in the midst of the forest. The iron gates were open and, judging by the depth of snow piled up against them, had been so since autumn. The grey sky was breeding more snow now and on either side the high outer fence stretched into the blurred distance, sagging in places. The watchtowers stood like tall black cranes, one of them with a dangerous list. Inside the wire, the huts were squat white shapes with here and there a misshapen one where the roof had collapsed. The doors at the ends, shielded by overhangs, were mostly shut but some sagged open on rotted hinges.

I told my driver to wait and keep the engine and heater running. Then I walked slowly through the gates. There were other footprints in the snow leading to the first hut, a larger H-shaped one which used to be the guardroom. Behind it was the inner fence with another set of open gates. Within that fence were the huts. The guardroom door opened before I reached it. I wasn't surprised. The sight of a shiny black ZiL and an official in a long black overcoat with a sable astrakhan and matching gloves was not a common one for the wretches within. A hunched figure hobbled out, muffled in old clothes and using a stick. He hurried over as if afraid to miss me.

'Greetings, greetings, I am Kholopov, Ivanovich Kholopov. I was sergeant here. I am your guide, if you wish.'

He had a thin dirty face and his lips were never still, working continuously. He looked smelly. I knew he would be, I knew exactly how he would smell, but I had no need to get that close.

'I know the camp well, I know everything about it, I have been here nearly thirty years. I worked here, I was sergeant of the guards.'

I took off one glove and fished out a few coins from my coat pocket. I didn't bother to count them.

He held out his hand, his glove worn through on the palm, and I dropped them into it without touching him.

'Thank you, thank you kindly. What would you like to see – the kitchen, the offices, the punishment cells, the graveyard, the huts, the bathhouse? It is all empty, all available.'

'Everything. Show me everything.'

That puzzled him. 'Of course, of course, I can show you every hut, every bunk. Only there are very many and it will take time—'

'I will tell you when to stop.' I noticed now that he had a twitch in his left cheek.

'With pleasure, it is pleasure. Please follow me.'

We crunched through the snow together, slowly because of the curious way he hobbled. He told me about the building of the camp in the 1930s, initially by the first prisoners sent to it who lived – and often died – in holes in the ground until the huts were up. He described its expansion, then its gradual contraction after the death of Stalin until its closure in the Gorbachev era, by which time it housed only a few politicals, as he called us.

'But when Comrade Gorbachev let the prisoners go the authorities forgot about us, the guards and administrators. We stayed, we had nowhere to go. How can we go anywhere? Where could we go? There is no work for us here but we cannot afford to move. Unless they open the camp again.' His laugh became a prolonged cough. 'We have pensions but they are a pittance, which is why we have to beg from generous visitors such as yourself.'

We reached the first of the huts inside the inner wire. The number one was still just visible in faded white on the wooden door. 'We can go in if you want but there is nothing there, nothing to see. They're all the same. In this block there are numbers one to thirty-nine, the rest are in the other block. Twenty prisoners to a hut but sometimes there were more. They are all the same, the huts. So were the prisoners. Over there are the camp offices and the punishment cells and the bathhouse and the sick bay and our own quarters. They are more interesting. These are just huts.'

I offered him a cigarette. He glanced as if to check that he had not misunderstood, then grabbed one. 'Thank you, thank you.' His eyes lingered on the packet, which he couldn't read because they were American, Peter Stuyvesant. His eyes lingered too on my gold lighter. 'Number thirty-seven,' I said. 'Take me to thirty-seven.'

The cigarette seemed to give him energy and his lop-sided hobble through the rows became more rapid. The smoke was good and pungent in the cold air.

'You see, they are all the same,' he said again when we reached it.

'Open it.'

I sensed he was reluctant, probably because of the effort involved. He put his cigarette between his lips, leaned his stick against the wall, pushed down on the handle and put his shoulder to the door. It was obviously stiff at first but then opened so freely that he nearly lost his balance. He stood back so that I could look in. 'Nothing to see, just the bunks. They're all the same.'

He had to move as I stepped in. It took a while for my eyes to adjust to the gloom. There were sprinklings of snow on the earth floor beneath the closed wooden window-hatches. The ceiling was low, the wooden double bunks lined the sides, some with broken slats, others still with remnants of old straw. The gangway down the middle was too narrow for two to walk side by side and to get between the bunks you had to go sideways. There was an old metal bucket on the floor by the door and a musty smell. It felt colder inside than out.

I walked two-thirds of the way down and stopped by the lower bunk on the left side. It was no different to all the others, of course. My guide hobbled behind me.

'You knew someone who was here?' he asked.

I didn't answer. After another minute or so of fruitless and circular contemplation, I turned back up the aisle. You live with the past but you can't live it. I left my guide struggling to close the door and headed back towards the gates. The snow was thicker now and the outlines of distant huts rapidly became indistinct. Eventually I heard him shuffling and panting and he caught up with me.

'Is there anything else – the punishment cells, the camp offices?'

I was between the inner and outer fences, approaching the H-shaped guardroom, when he made one last effort, pointing with his stick. 'I could show you the cookhouse. We use it. It still has the ovens and pots and pans—'

That made me stop and think. 'No,' I said. 'That was the guards' cookhouse. The cookhouse for the prisoners was that one, there.' I pointed at a long low building just inside the inner fence.

He followed my gaze, then looked back at me, his lips still for once. 'You are right. I had forgotten. I have been here too long, I am too familiar. But you, how could you—'

'I was here.'

We stared at each other in a long silence, but for the hiss of the snow. Those three words, three simple words, sunk into him like stones in a pond. Who were the prisoners, the real prisoners? And how could I be a senior official with a ZiL and furs? I took the cigarettes and the remaining coins from my pocket. He dropped his stick in the snow and held out his cupped hands. He was still staring, uncomprehending, as my car pulled away.

At the foot of the original Russian text was a hand-written note in English, in Badger's characteristic forward-sloping hand and his usual brown ink: *So you see, Charles, we are all prisoners really, even the guards. Tell your people who doubt my motivation – is this not enough?*

Charles closed that volume of Josef's file and put it with its mate. Then he picked up Badger's file, a slim single volume also buff-coloured but this time with a red stripe, a different number system and a white stick-on label with heavy black lettering saying, 'Closed. Do not digitise.' He had stuck that on himself years before, proof of rare premonition. It meant the case had remained secret and, unlike digitised files, was fully recoverable.

LEGACY

CHARLES THOROUGHGOOD #2

Charles Thoroughgood, hero of Alan Judd's classic
A Breed of Heroes, has left the army to be trained
by MI6 in the arts of the Cold War.

Nothing could prepare him, however, for the
unexpected inheritance left him by his late father,
which leads him back into an old school friendship
with Viktor, a Russian diplomat living in London, and
beyond that into the murky world of Soviet espionage
at the height of the nuclear threat to the West ...

**SIMON &
SCHUSTER**